PRAISE FOR *SCAR TISSUE*

"This persuasive and dizzying novel grabs you and doesn't let go. It is sexy, disturbing and relentless. What it says about human nature will keep you up at night. It's also constantly entertaining and unnervingly passionate. *Scar Tissue* is amazing and weird in all the best ways."

—Fred Leebron, author of *Six Figures*,
Out West, and *Welcome to Christiania* n

"*Scar Tissue* has all that we've come to expect from Jeff Hess's crime fiction—sweat-soaked Florida settings, uncompromising authenticity, and wild plots with hairpin turns—but adds yet another layer of ground-in grit. Hess's new protagonists, Dylan and Abby, are damaged goods—selfish, yet sympathetic, slick cons, but also lost souls—and, most importantly, complicated women who are written and treated by Hess as such. In his latest, Hess spills just as much blood as in his previous novels, but it's in the scars still healing where the real story lies."

—Steph Post, author of *Miraculum*, *Lightwood*,
Walk in the Fire, and *Holding Smoke*

"This gritty novel is the redheaded stepchild of *Martyrs* mated with *Thelma and Louise*—layers of darkness, vengeance, and chaos wrapped tightly together into a ball of sinuous fury."

—Richard Thomas, author of *Disintegration*
and *Breaker* (Thriller Award nominee)

SCAR TISSUE

BOOKS BY JEFFERY HESS

Novels
Scar Tissue
Roughhouse
Tushhog
Beachhead
No Salvation
Scar Tissue

Story Collection
Cold War Canoe Club

Anthologies (as editor)
Home of the Brave: Stories in Uniform
Home of the Brave: Somewhere in the Sand

JEFFERY HESS

SCAR TISSUE

Down & Out Books
3959 Van Dyke Road, Suite 265
Lutz, FL 33558
DownAndOutBooks.com

The characters and events in this book are fictitious. Any similarity to real persons, living or dead, is coincidental and not intended by the author.

Cover design by Zach McCain

ISBN: 1-64396-267-1
ISBN-13: 978-1-64396-267-2

A voice said, Look me in the stars
And tell me truly, men of earth,
If all the soul-and-body scars
Were not too much to pay for birth.
—*Robert Frost*

My candle burns at both ends;
It will not last the night:
But ah, my foes, and oh, my friends-
It gives a lovely light!
—*Edna St. Vincent Millay*

One

Every April 9th Dylan Rivers finds herself in bed with a woman she barely knows. This year, the bed is in a budget motel on the opposite side of Tampa Bay. The woman with her is a chew toy with no modesty and a body like a model. They'd met a few hours earlier at the Pinellas Pub, from which she followed Dylan back to this shit hole. The stench of mildew stabs in her nose, but it's not the reason she's holding her breath as the woman does her thing between Dylan's legs. Breath holding is a habit she began as a child while hiding from beatings meted out by her father. Now though, with her hands wrapped in the woman's hair, Dylan's lungs are swollen in her ribcage and threaten to burst. With her head thrown back and her breath clamped off, her vision blurs, but she won't let herself enjoy it too much. And she will *not* reciprocate. Pleasuring this woman is not remotely her goal. She's neither Dylan's lover nor her partner, not her wife or girlfriend. She means nothing more to Dylan than any other ingredient in her recipe for the ritual.

The throbbing in her chest becomes syncopated with the woman's chin brushing across the sheets beneath them. The beat keeps her patient, helps her stay the course. To Dylan, life is not a car on a highway, but rather a train on tracks. Except for today. Today is her birthday. Her fortieth. Today, she allows herself one derailment...but not yet.

Women Dylan's age have sons in high school, some entering college. Women her age celebrate this milestone birthday with

3

tombstone replicas in their front yards and surprise parties where friends wear black and roast the woman of honor. Women her age have husbands in linen suits who order roses and break out hidden gifts like new cars and jewelry to thunderous applause from all in attendance. Dylan received no gifts or hugs today. Her gift to herself will be the pleasure of a blade when she has the proper conditions in which to utilize it. Until then, she goes about her business, getting to the brink, but no farther, with this woman.

Abby Stratton had danced into the Pinellas Pub earlier that night with her friends Brittney, Star, and Loretta. Girls' night out. The band played a fusion of house and reggae music, amps cranked, making the sticky floor quake beneath Abby's feet as they navigated a maze of pool tables. They all wore blue jeans and high heels and the world became their dance floor. Abby hadn't been out with the girls in the weeks since she'd hooked up with Vince—an artsy, graduate-school kid who wore black almost exclusively, even in the brutal Florida heat. He had all the makings of a prospect, but had fallen apart before she got what she wanted from him. Now though, with only three weeks until her deadline, she carried eleven thousand dollars in traveler's checks in her purse, more than enough to get her and that special someone to Burma. She just needed to find the right person.

While her friends had rent to make and drugs to buy and procedures to have, Abby's freedom allowed her to disappear for a month or more at a time. All the girls thought she volunteered for the International Red Cross, and Abby never discouraged them from that assumption. No good could come from them learning what she planned.

The far side of the bar hung in shadows without the strobes and spotlights swirling around. In the dim light, she made her way through the crowd. Nobody caught her eye right away, so she kept walking to the far end of the place, where cold air spiked her nipples and made Abby hug herself for a moment as she approached the bar. Then she saw a candidate—a woman with her back to the action, alone, not scanning the room or dancing in her seat. That told Abby all she needed to know. She'd found a perfect prospect.

Abby wanted to slip into the restroom to check herself, but instead resorted to the mirror lining the wall behind the bar. Over the curves of tequila bottles, she smoothed her hair into place, and near the vodka bottles she checked her lipstick. With the woman in her periphery, hope cascaded over Abby in that instant. Even from that distance, Abby felt this alluring woman had what it took to be her accomplice.

As she approached, Abby noticed the woman wore dark pants, wide at the ankles, and a tucked-in shirt, as if she'd just come from work. A desk job, perhaps. Her shoulders and back looked athletic, as if she played sports. Maybe college gymnastics. As she got closer, the woman's pants were jeans, not trousers. But instead of thick leather boots, she wore sensible lady loafers propped upon the stool's footrail. Perhaps management somewhere, Abby thought. No matter. The woman's naked ring finger suggested either she was single or she wanted everyone to think so. She wore her hair pulled back and her posture was erect, which made Abby guess off-duty cop or perhaps military from what they called CENTCOM at the air base. She appeared to be alone, which could mean friendless, unworthy of knowing, or unknowable.

Without turning, the woman said, "Your drink's on me."

The music blared, even on this side of the bar away from the dance floor, but Abby heard her clearly. "Stoli and pineapple," Abby said without hesitation. She hadn't bought her own drink in a bar since she was sixteen. "You're not married, are you? Or a cop?"

The woman chewed ice from her drink, then hit her cigarette, deep, and looked at the glowing end. Abby hoped she'd stub it out on her extended tongue, all the while holding that intense eye contact with her. But she didn't. "Why?" the woman asked.

"Should I be?"

Abby couldn't pin down her nationality. She had thick, dark hair with a medium-dark complexion, but there were no telltale signs around her eyes or nose. She assumed the woman's ancestry involved some sort of hyphenated American thing, though Abby wouldn't bet on it, nor did it matter. The dark tones of her hair and the sharpness of her blue eyes reminded Abby of a holiday in Estonia a number of years ago. "Unbelievable," Abby said with her hand resting on the woman's leg. They drank without speaking. The woman looked even better than she needed to, and Abby said, "You don't have to be suave with me. This isn't a job interview; it's an audition for a part."

The motel bed is against the wall, enveloped in an eerie canopy of shadows where the room feels ten degrees warmer than when they'd started. Despite friction and the fluids they've exchanged, the woman smells of perfume and liquor, highlighted by that funk of mold in the room. After three rounds of breath holding, Dylan gulps down a big wad of the dank motel room air. Her lungs are heavy and wet. Five minutes go by. She feels the pressure build again in her distended lungs until she can take it no longer and exhales the trapped fog as she collapses her legs onto the bed. The woman climbs up Dylan's torso, huddles there, both gasping for new wind. It's the best Dylan can do to simulate an orgasm in her effort to satisfy this woman's sense of duty or ego. Acting is more pragmatic than trying to explain she only comes when she cuts.

Dylan rolls to her side. The sound of bells fills the room as a train crosses the intersection at the end of the parking lot. This is followed by two blasts of its horn as it continues, staying on schedule.

"You are amazing," the woman says, snuggling up to Dylan, who lies there like sexual roadkill. Abby's legs are crossed at the ankles, her arms out to the side, exposed, showing herself to this stranger in visual confession, like she does every year. One arm dangles off the bed and the other rests under the woman as she drapes Dylan's left side. The sheets are crumpled and saturated with sweat. They're sharing the wet spot—what otherwise might be fluids of contentment.

The woman traces her thumbnail along the jagged edges of the scar on Dylan's chest and, as their breathing calms, her other fingers roam aimlessly and brush across her nipples. She resists the urge to stroke the woman back with the tips of her own fingers and instead concentrates on the sweat dripping from her face onto her chest. Her breasts push into Dylan's ribs and their legs entwine. Dylan wants her to stay, but she needs her to go. She is nothing more than a delay, yet her head tingles with the notion of keeping the woman near a while longer.

"How'd you get this scar?"

No one's ever asked before. The others had all pretended the scars weren't there, which allowed her to expose them all the more—confession without conversation. This woman has no right to ask. No right to know.

A dim glow of passing headlights sweeps across the ceiling through the smoke-soaked curtains. Dylan cranes her head away when the car sounds close enough to come through the wall. A moment later, taillights cast the room in a red glow. Just another U-turn.

Lying there, Dylan repeats the woman's question in her mind and recognizes her lack of emphasis on any single word. The question was breathed without the serrated edge of judgment, and that allows Dylan to relax a little, though she still doesn't want to answer. Post-coital sharing will only add to the delay, and she really should be gone by now.

She had been a hair puller when Dylan went through the motions on top of her. Dylan had felt her sides being touched, the woman's arms and legs randomly scissoring her. But she can't be positive if the woman raked her hands up and down her torso during the deed, if she'd felt the remnants of all her previous rituals. Maybe she just imagined it, but it felt as if the woman kind of read her scars like Braille, tracing intently enough to draw blood with those sharp, fake nails.

Dylan's in no mood to explain. She'd rather lie there, floating in the obscurity between sleep and consciousness for the brief period she'll indulge it.

The woman is maybe half Dylan's age. She can't tell for sure and not that it matters. If it wasn't her, it would be someone similar to her. Roughly the same age, the same build. Her appeal resides in her looks, yes, but not in the traditional sense of the word. There's no glamour perpetuated by her hair or makeup, though her jeans and T-shirt looked tailor made. A pink rubber band held back her hair. The curves at her jaw, just beneath her ears, excited Dylan. The woman commanded attention, but she didn't demand it. Perhaps her friends had put her up to approaching Dylan in the bar earlier. Her girlfriends seemed yoked to the act of artificial effort, while Abby roamed naturally. Clean. Unobstructed. That is what amazed Dylan the most.

Every year, Dylan hooked up with somebody. The feat carried no high-five, bragging rights bullshit. Just a means to an end. Blonde or brunette, top-heavy or straight as a wall, it never mattered. Each woman was only as memorable as a sandwich eaten when hungry—sustenance. Good, but not momentous. A mystic sense of duality had separated this one from the field of painted faces in the bar earlier—designer goods at a flea market. And she'd sent signals, steady bursts of invisible flares as she approached Dylan from the far reaches of her peripheral vision. Some sort of force drew them together from opposite sides of the bar. Magnetism. Charged particles in twisted meridian—coupling imminent, though temporary.

Now, Dylan's legs twitch sporadically, which keeps her from drifting off. She's not practiced in conversation, especially pillow talk. If she keeps quiet long enough, maybe the woman will drop it.

"This must have been deep as hell," she says, tapping the

scar with a blunt nail.

That nail. Even in the room's darkness, the polish is as chipped and faded as the paint on all the shitty houses Dylan had grown up in. The woman slows her fingers and stops in the center of the scar, as if to concentrate. The old cicatrix is forever jagged from infection and neglect all those years ago, and she'd learned about moisturizer too late to do that one any good.

"It's a long story."

"Seriously," the woman says, lifting her head from Dylan's shoulder and pancaking it on the pillow to face her. "Tell me how you got this one."

Her breath smells like it tastes.

"Let's just say it's a remnant of a broken heart."

"Oh, really?" The woman's voice perks up a scale.

Though freshly and thoroughly fucked, she has a full head of enthusiasm, which surprises Dylan.

The woman's keeping Dylan from cold metal cutting into the hot meat of her lower abdomen, that tender real estate occupying the space between the waistband and left front pocket of her jeans. She's horny for the slicing, the bleeding, and best of all, the release the ritual provides.

"This scar is epic," the woman says. "Tell me how you got it."

Heaving her legs over the side of the bed and finding the floor with her feet, Dylan sits for a second and lights a cigarette, then pitches it toward the plastic ashtray. "Stop, alright!"

"No, I'm serious. I think there's something to these scars. They're a map of some sort."

"Get the fuck out of here. A map? It's just random shit that was in my head. I didn't know what I was doing."

"But don't you see? This scar is like a sundial." She points toward Dylan's thigh. "And this one is like a compass, and this one here is so definitely an ax and yet..." She leans back. "When you see them from a certain distance, it forms like a big picture made of little pictures. Kind of like a Chuck Close painting."

Dylan imagines killing her. Greasing her. Icing her. Imagines

9

being puffed up like a mad woman, all frothing outrage and insanity, clobbering her over the head and throwing her into her trunk. Or chopping her up in the bathtub and shoveling her into Glad bags, piece by piece. "It's time for you to go."

"What?"

"Look," Dylan says, "just because we fucked, we're not a couple."

The woman doesn't flinch. "Damn, girl, relax. I'm here for a *good* time, not a *long* time."

Dylan unscrews the cap on a water bottle and raises it toward the door. "Just go."

"I don't think you understand—"

"No! You don't understand." Dylan spins and points in her face. "It's not like you have a choice here."

Instead of getting pissed and leaving, the woman acts like she heard different words. She rolls onto her back and says, "Maybe in the morning we can go get brunch."

Her bare legs are together now, a tiny swatch of hair just visible at the top; but Dylan's done with her, and she feels she'll burn up if this bitch doesn't disappear.

Standing there naked, Dylan squares her shoulders. "Don't make me be an asshole."

"You *are* being an asshole." The woman spreads her arms, as if to display the bed as evidence. "You really want me to leave?"

Next year, Dylan will try to find a mute. She nods. "Seriously," she says, her firmness absolute. "Go on, get out of here."

When the woman finally swallows the hint, or her pride, she surges in spastic motions. Reaching, bending to pick up her belongings from the soiled carpet. She sets the armload on top of the dark dresser. "You know, a do-and-ditch doesn't seem your style. You really should let me help you figure out what those scars are a map of. You might be surprised."

"Wrap it up," Dylan says.

* * *

10

Abby slides on her jeans and T-shirt without putting on her bra or thong, straps on her high Lucite shoes before scooping her underwear and purse off the top of the dresser. She storms out, meaning to slam the door with all her strength and punctuate her departure, but the damn thing opens in and the knob is slippery. When the door shuts behind her, the effect is little more than someone in a hurry.

A numbing haze of fatigue washes over her. She can't rush to her car with hostility because her limbs might as well be cardboard as she struggles, walking around the sensitivity between her thighs. Swallows back the sting of emotions from being dismissed. Of being wronged, and plain wrong.

Halfway to her car, she turns, praying Dylan isn't watching from the window. She can't see her, so she just assumes she's there and the humiliation factor rises exponentially.

Abby holds her underwear and purse awkwardly in one arm and snatches open the Jetta's door, squinting at the light filling the car. She never locks the doors because she always leaves the keys in the ignition.

She flops into the driver's seat, hugging her belongings on her lap, and pulls the door shut awkwardly with her right hand. Her vision glows red from the flashing arrow on the motel sign. As the engine turns over, the stereo kicks on and Janice Joplin's voice fills the car with "Turtle Blues." CD cases lie strewn about the passenger seat and floorboard—The Doors, Jimi Hendrix, Nirvana—but this one is her favorite because the torment in the song helps her think.

It's too late to start from scratch again tonight. She thinks about the traveler's checks in her purse. She should just go to the airport and begin her pilgrimage, continue her search for the right one along the way.

Anger causes saliva to boil into the back of her throat, juices rising in her esophagus as she balls her fists. She is usually an excellent judge of character. Dylan seemed such a perfect partner for her plan, all the elements and then some. Abby's sure she can use Dylan's scars against her. Not by blackmail, but by convincing her they are clues that will reveal answers to all of life's questions. But she can't force her. Can't even be sure she'll ever see her again—Dylan banished her. It was over. Fuck it. She decides right then to drive to the airport.

As she shifts from P to R, she thinks of Dylan again. Them in bed together, those scars, and the hard time she had with Abby's zipper. The more she'd tugged, the more intense her face got. Abby smiles, shifting from R to D, and pulls out of the motel parking lot while recalling the expression on her face—concentration as if splitting an atom. That face couldn't belong to someone shallow.

In bed, questions had filled her mind as she'd touched Dylan. All those welts she'd felt, those scars, she knew they weren't random. Those hadn't come from a car crash or from falling out of a tree as a kid. Obviously. Abby could tell the older scars from the newer by the way the raised skin felt on hers.

She takes back roads, slowly, with the intention of making her way to Starkey Road so she can cross over and get to Tampa International with as little delay as possible.

Motionless at a stoplight, she is under the spell of exhaustion, yet the energy and emotion in Janis Joplin's voice makes Abby's skin itch with tingles.

She's thinking of nothing other than dying. Every time she thinks of death it's like a flash of lightning, but the thunder stays with her longer than other thoughts. This plan for death is something she's never questioned. She's accepted the challenge, and time is running out. She has only eighteen days left before the deadline she is adamant about meeting.

She throws the bundle she's still holding into the passenger seat. A metal-on-metal sound makes her look in time to see a silver key hanging from an old-fashioned brass motel tag as it clangs off the seat belt connector. It falls between the seat and the console, and she reaches to retrieve it. As the light turns green, she extends her foot to the gas pedal.

The posture isn't ideal for driving and she can't readily retrieve the key, but she's driven under worse circumstances, hundreds of times, overseas mostly—Haiti, Thailand, Zimbabwe. Dangerous places full of damage and despair always seem like logical choices for finding the right one among the talent pool of those stripped of all human pride. Yet, some of the most damaged people she's ever met were doing the most good. Amongst those broken soldiers and Peace Corps volunteers she found a few willing to kill her, or themselves, but none willing to do both, though she did come close that time with Derek in Bosnia. In between trips, she tried her luck with cops and firefighters around town.

As she extracts the key from beneath the seat, she thinks first of revenge, but then considers the happenstance of fate. They're meant to be together. In her crouched posture, arm bent on the passenger seat, she jerks the wheel through a rough U-turn.

By Dylan's normal standards, the dingy bathroom in this shitty motel in the dirty part of town wouldn't be acceptable, but she's comfortable today amid the mold and broken tile and cheap motel towels. It feels familiar, and the electric hiss of the florescent light fixture calms her.

She stands at the vanity in the motel bathroom, ignoring the mirror, and opens her traveling shower kit. The smell of soap and leather wafts to her nose and reminds her of the baseball glove she kept under her pillow as a kid. She removes a plastic soap holder, travel-size bottles of shampoo and generic conditioner, brown vial of Anbesol, disposable razor, perfume, brush, and her solid deodorant. Each of these items has its proper place in the main compartment, but she sets them aside now and feels inside for the familiar crosshatch in the handle of her venerated X-ACTO knife.

It's not there.

"Fuck." She checks all horizontal surfaces. Beside the sink, deodorant is lined up behind hair mousse, which is right in front of her perfume. Her comb lies lengthwise in the bristles of her upturned brush.

She knows she didn't forget the X-ACTO.

Standing at the sink, her muscles shake in isometric clench. She opens a drawer on the left side of the towel bar. The drawer is empty and sudden panic speeds though her. How could she not account for that most important item? She slams the drawer and yanks it open again, then a third time, but still nothing is there. She bends to one knee and looks on the floor, but it isn't there either. She stands and catches her reflection in the mirror. For a split second, she mistakes it for somebody else in the room with her. She jumps in reaction, not recognizing herself— her hair a little grayer, a little thinner at the ends—but wastes no time in resuming her search for the blade. If she can't find it, the ritual she's maintained for the past twenty-five years will be ruined. Tonight is supposed to be number twenty-six.

Skipping it is not an option, no matter how much she wishes she could.

There are other methods.

She'd used a steak knife at sixteen and a pair of scissors the next year. Three years later, she used a piece of clear glass from a broken bottle of orange soda she drank before smashing it into a wall. Glass cuts well enough, but the X-ACTO is precise and always on the top of the list. After this much time, she's convinced there is no benefit to improvising. Omitting steps in her ritual is like pulling bricks from condemned buildings.

She unfolds the bag's hinges farther to reveal the tiny zipper sewn into the lining of the shower kit. She unzips it, and the familiar knurling of the silver X-ACTO between her fingers makes relief sigh out of her. It's not like her to misplace something, especially something so important, but today, nerves being what they are, she doesn't analyze it.

Blade now firmly in hand, she eases her naked body down onto the closed lid of the toilet and feels the cold surface on her bare buttocks. She reaches toward the countertop beside her and grabs the small bottle of Anbesol. She holds it in her fingers, studies it. Not as if it were an antidote to infection, but more like an intrusion on the natural order. After sprinkling a small amount on her lower abdomen, she wets the blade of the X-ACTO knife for antisepsis and then inhales and exhales deeply to cleanse her mind, to calm her excitement.

Leaning back, her flesh absorbs the coolness of the porcelain tank and it adds to the stimulation. In that position, she waits until the contact between skin and tank renders both surfaces tepid.

The blade shimmers in the glare of the fluorescent light directly overhead. She lowers her arm, letting the blade touch skin made tender from being covered first by diapers, then denim, then military fatigues, then business suits. Slightly, as if a fallen feather landing on beach sand, metal makes contact with flesh. The blade is silent, but she feels the sizzle of heat meeting cool anticipation. She draws the blade from her stomach to her thigh, slowly, with the dull edge, grazing it side to side, then in circles. Teasing. Savoring. Building. The Tantric method of self-cutting. In that moment of delayed gratification, Dylan drifts through the fog of other women on other birthdays. She's never been able to recall the first time, and doesn't waste time considering it now. She lives for the bleeding yet to come.

Her hand sweeps the blade across the skin of her pelvis. Again, her discipline pays dividends. When she feels that magical instant of *NOW*, she squeezes her fingers, bends her wrist with increasing force, and presses the sharp edge of the blade to make a slow, deliberate cut. She twists the blade through her skin, feeling the sting of metal parting flesh, etching the new design. All the while, she pretends another person's hand guides the blade. Etching, then scoring, she cuts her specific design. Though not an elaborate pattern, it carries greater meaning.

The idea fell into her mind while sitting at the bar that night. She usually couldn't think of anything until she had the blade in hand, but this seemed so right. A sideways eight, the symbol of infinity. It forms a twisted, but never-ending line that increases without limit. She goes slowly, ensuring depth while maintaining the pattern. Flaring the ends, keeping the center narrow—not risking it looking like just two circles together. Over and over, just as the symbol represents, she slices in the pattern, deeper and darker with each pass, wondering if she can hit vital organs if she goes deep.

This pain may not be enough.

The gauze of contempt clouding her everyday vision lifts from her eyes. Clarity refreshes, awakens her with rewards unavailable elsewhere. The oxygen rushing into her lungs turns the blood from blue to red several layers beneath her flesh. This one will scar brilliantly when the platelets heal the tissue.

She sits on the closed toilet lid, all tension eased and anxiety gone, as blood flows in little rivers over her hip. She feasts on the erotic pleasure of it all. Her engorged clitoris throbs; her nipples are erect, drawing even more blood away from her brain. A few side-to-side strokes with her blood-smeared finger, that's all she needs. And she explodes.

Her head falls back against the wall as her central nervous system releases. Mouth open, her lips struggle to curve upward. This is her attempt at a smile, a true smile; the only one for the better part of a fucking year.

She toys with the blood, widens the trails until an edge water-falls onto the floor. After a moment, she dips an index finger into the blood and draws a large A on her abdomen in honor of Abby. Last year, if memory serves, it had been a K, but the actual name escapes her.

She reaches down, touches the growing puddle on the cracked tile floor, before rising to step a pace closer to the sink. With the stroke of a child finger painting, she draws an inverted anchor on the mirror with her blood. A fuck you to her Navy lifer-father. Despite the shaky artistry, the effort taxes her, leaves her breathless. She collapses back onto the commode. The tank is still warm against her back. Here she feels whole. Serene. Everything is perfect.

Without knocking, Abby lets herself in with the key she inadvertently picked up. Upon entering, the room's old-bar-in-the-morning smell registers and she's surprised she didn't notice it the first time she entered earlier. Now though, the scent of beer stains turned to mold, unwashed linens, and the musk of sex is everywhere. The room would be dark if not for the blue glow from the television tuned to Telemundo, where accordion music and voices in Spanish blare. It's a talk show or a game show, Abby can't be sure, and she can't figure out what they might be celebrating, but it's a party wherever they're broadcasting from. She lowers the volume and notices Dylan isn't in bed. This surprises Abby. Most people can't stay awake after she's finished with them.

Through the chiaroscuro fog in the room, a wedge of light projects from the partially opened bathroom door. She strains her ear as she walks toward it, focusing to hear anything coming from the opposite side. The mystery of what's behind the door pulls her closer. An intoxicating frisson of thought coursing to a lump in her throat. She wants to cycle through the list of possibilities of what she might see, but doesn't want to suffer the delay. Instead, one eye winks shut as she strains her face toward the small gap of light coming through.

Nothing. She can't see her.

The cry of the hinges as she opens the door jolts through her like a fire alarm, but it's impossible to stop herself until her shoulder recoils as the door hits its stop.

Despite the brightness of the overhead lights, the room pulses in an orange haze and she doesn't know why until she sees the floor. "Fuck. Shit. Oh, my God." Her voice shakes out of her. "What have you done?" Her immediate thought is *she's opened a vein in a suicide attempt.*

Dylan's eyes are almost shut, but they snap open when Abby says, "Fuck. That's a lot of blood. Is it fatal?"

Dylan stares back at her, but not the way she stared when they'd met.

Abby makes no effort to move, to provide aid or judgment of any kind; she simply stands there, looking at Dylan. Seeing her naked again, but now through the haze of uncertain light, a taste of metal coats her tongue and she can't swallow it away. Dylan's entire soul lies exposed to her. Her nude figure, sitting there on the toilet, the blood painted on her abdomen and on the mirror. Murky, maroon blood spread out on the floor, seeping into the grout of the cracked tile like a copper-smelling mosaic. The more she looks at her, the less she thinks this wound is fatal, and she decides the reason for the scars is ceremonial. In that instant, she thinks Dylan is majestic, sitting there surrounded by her malignancy. She appears to be breathing fine, but looks weak.

Abby says, "You are *so* the right person for me."

Dylan raises herself in slow motion, as if the toilet seat levitates her. When she makes it to her feet, Abby notices something in her hand. From the doorway it looked like a pen, but now she recognizes that it has a blade. It looks like a scalpel, and Dylan's grip on it tightens, from tool to weapon. Once fully upright, she wades through the viscosity of her blood, smearing it with her bare feet, inching toward Abby. As she steps, her face loses all semblance of its previous ecstasy. The blood loss and resultant lack of oxygen to her brain seems to have affected her like an acid-high gone wrong. Her expression hardens.

Abby should step back, but she doesn't move, doesn't speak. The combination of the knife and Dylan's obvious anger causes absolute stillness. But, even with adrenaline coursing through her, no hairs raise on her neck, no fight or flight response makes her want to run. She looks at Dylan, not spiritually, but in a practical way, like having a conversation. Conducting business.

Dylan raises the X-ACTO knife from down by the side of her leg to her waist, pointing at Abby. A primordial hunter ready to attack her prey. But then her shoulders drop and she exhales. Abby doesn't know if she's taken something, or if she's whacked out strictly from blood loss.

"You're not going to hurt me," Abby says. "You love me."

Dylan looks at the knife, then at Abby. She lets it drop. It lands with a *clink* on the blood-covered tile and she sinks to her knees, kneeling in her blood as she slowly inches herself closer to Abby. Dylan reaches her arms up to grasp Abby's waist, then pulls her closer and buries her face in Abby's hip before losing consciousness.

"Great," Abby says, hugging Dylan's sweaty head to her thigh, watching herself smile in the blood-smeared mirror in front of her.

Abby eases Dylan onto the floor and tucks a hand towel under her head. The light from the bathroom casts Dylan in a center stage glow. Her naked torso sits at an incongruous angle and her wound bleeds onto the tile-side of the doorway. In that position, she's no longer the aggressor Abby's seen her to be. She's no longer the lover, either. She looks, of all things, peaceful lying there. Her hair appears gray in the light. In the bar earlier, Abby had guessed their ages as close together, but now she looks easily ten years older.

When she's sure Dylan's all the way out, she spreads her legs and looks at the fleshy welts across her pelvis and on both thighs. She surveys flesh made jagged by many such evenings. Lifts one of Dylan's arms to get a closer look at a cluster of scarring inside her biceps. Abby's suddenly jealous of the other women Dylan's been with before cutting. She wonders if she's the first to catch her—to find her, like buried treasure.

The air conditioner kicks on and the noise of it startles Abby. She grabs all but the last towel stuffed into the coiled rack and wipes blood off Dylan, cleans her as well as she can and in the process explores the old scars on her legs.

The big A finger-painted onto her torso requires too much attention and time, so Abby leaves her like this, sprawled across the threshold, half on tile and half on moldy bedroom carpet. She looks smaller now than she did in the bar, and in bed. Not little but reduced. The way old people are small.

Abby doesn't know what to do with her, but knows she can't leave Dylan there to get caught or bleed to death. All that blood, like block letters in red ink spelling out an urgent SOS or Mayday or whatever signal people in trouble use these days.

The wound isn't really that deep, and the flow already seems to be tapering off beneath the towel she left folded there. As she looks down at Dylan, naked and numb, calling an ambulance seems both unnecessary and like a betrayal.

After grabbing the last towel from the rack and draping it over her shoulder, Abby tightens her abdomen to support her back, and then bends down and grabs her under the arms. Even in four-inch heels, Abby's able to squat down until her jeans cut creases into the backs of her knees and make her wish she'd taken the time to put her underwear back on because the jeans are doing the same to her crotch. She grunts through the lift—like an Olympian hefting record weight—and gets Dylan into a sitting position. "You don't look it, but you're heavy as a church."

She tries lifting Dylan again, this time in a bear hug. With Dylan's weight crushing down on her, Abby only manages three steps backward before her knee buckles, throwing her off balance. She holds Dylan up by shifting all the weight to her other foot, but as she tries to right herself, one of Abby's four-inch heels rolls inward. She chirps like a muscle car skipping second gear from the shock of the pain and before she can recover, she crumbles to the floor with Dylan on top of her. Dylan's head misses the corner of the dresser by only inches, thudding on the carpet like a frozen turkey. Abby's wind has not been knocked out of her, but for a moment she lies there feeling the warmth radiating from her ankle and wonders if it's broken.

"Don't be broken. Please, don't be broken."

Abby rolls Dylan off her with a strong shove and Dylan's dead weight flops over, landing face up.

Now, Abby can really see the scars. Each tells a story, but she isn't interested in what they have to say anymore. With time running out, she's only interested in using the scars to her persuasive end. And there is much material to draw from. Where Dylan's paleness is carved with detail, the only alteration to the aging skin she displays is the memory of coloration by the sun. She covets Dylan's pain, but curses her own.

Sitting on the bed, Abby unbuckles her shoe, grabs her foot, and works the ankle back-to-front and side-to-side. The easy movement relieves her, but picking Dylan up again isn't something she looks forward to—just thinking about it makes her ankle seem stiff. She makes it to her feet and stands crookedly, one foot in a shoe and one flat on the floor. She raises herself back up to heel-height, looks at the shoe on the floor, then sits on the edge of the bed to take off the other shoe.

Unable to accept defeat, she soldiers on. Looking for an alternative, she checks outside, where the concrete walkway is cold and feels wet beneath her bare feet. Down the breezeway, between a peeling stucco wall and an out of order Coke machine, she catches a flash of weather-beaten brass illuminated by light from the parking lot. It's a luggage cart that, judging by the sag in the platform and the angle of the wheels, hasn't been used in quite a while. The heavy-gauge carpet covering the platform is slimy with humidity but it will serve the purpose.

One of the wheels has a rusty bearing and it squeals every other revolution. Abby tries to silence the noise by shifting the weight onto the other three wheels as she rolls by open windows. At the door to their room, she wheels the cart into a position obliquely to hold the door open. She then straddles Dylan, one bare foot on each side of her and hefts her up by the armpits again, this time wrestling her aboard the luggage cart.

Once Dylan's in place, Abby cools her pounding head on the cart's cold brass pole and catches her breath before taking hold of the cart and her platform shoes in one hand, using the other to tug the door closed by the key she'd left in the lock when she let herself in.

Dylan's dead weight on the luggage cart silences the squeaking wheel, making it less conspicuous for Abby to haul this unconscious and naked woman down the open corridor and into the parking lot. The pavement under her bare feet is no longer smooth. It cuts like broken glass as gravity bears down from the burden of tugging the luggage cart. At the car, the passenger-side door opens less than smoothly, and she has to swat debris off the passenger seat before she lugs Dylan up. Wrestling her into the seat is difficult with her sore ankle, but she stuffs Dylan in and folds the towel over her naked pelvis, using the seat belt to apply pressure. The poor bitch is turning grayish-green, like old dollar bills.

With Dylan loaded into the car, Abby wheels the luggage cart between the dumpster and a rusted Camaro on the near side of the lot. She checks over her shoulder on her way around the car, trusting any witnesses at that time of night are not the type to get involved.

In the car, she fishes her cell phone out from her purse and hits the speed-dial button for her house, then looks over at Dylan, whose head rests against the window, eyes closed in a peaceful pose. After three rings, Abby says into the phone, "Hey, you're there? Good. Listen, I'm bringing somebody back. Yeah." She pauses. "No. It's a woman. I need your help. She's bleeding."

Two

After treating Dylan's wound with a couple of butterfly strips, gauze pad, and white tape, Lawton pulls the covers up to Dylan's chin. She's a good-looking woman. Probably mid-thirties, he guesses. Didn't appear that she ever had kids. Or, maybe she had them young. Either way, she projects fitness. Pale as Styrofoam, but toned. Not unpleasant to look at, but he couldn't shake his disgust of the scars, which remind him of Bradbury's *The Illustrated Man*. And while this fuels his disappointment over Abby's choice of companion, absent is any semblance of shock. He won't make any comments or give Abby a hard time because it won't do any good, and there is no need to piss her off. She's long had a penchant for dangerous men—she always seems to find those on the brink of self-destruction—but every once in a while it's an equally fucked-up woman. Like this one. Abby's come home with a number of clinically depressed geniuses and bed-wetting alcoholics in the past, so a comatose cutter with a decent body is not bad by comparison. But still.

He'd had to leave a big-tittied blonde with a tequila buzz to help Abby with this. He *had* to—he owes her. Would, in fact, do anything she asks, as she would do for him. As they have always done.

Early the next morning, Lawton makes his way to the motel on Park Boulevard despite his hangover. There are a thousand destinations he'd rather be heading toward. He scratches at his beard stubble with one hand as the other rests on the steering wheel.

At the motel, Lawton grabs a bucket of cleaning supplies from the back of his truck and uses the key Abby gave him to let himself into room number 9. With the handle of the bucket cutting into the palm of his hand, all he can think about is the time he heard The Beatles' *White Album* played backward in his friend Dave's living room back in high school: "Number nine, number nine, number nine…"

Lawton pulls up his headphones and blasts Metallica as a way to distract himself from the horror awaiting him on the other side of the door.

His sister and the cutter left in a hurry, and all the evidence of their union lay exposed before him. Rumpled sheets, the smell of sex, an open bottle of water next to an ash tray, and a pack of cigarettes wait for the torrid couple to return—after an intimate shower, perhaps. On the chair in the corner sit the cutter's neatly folded clothes. He knows Abby to be incapable of folding laundry, so assumes the cutter is OCD or something. Lawton finds a pair of sensible shoes under the chair, but no purse. He checks under the bed. Nothing. He lifts the folded clothes hoping to find it underneath, but instead feels something heavy in the folded clothes. He sets them down and pulls out a wallet from the pants' back pocket. He reads "Safe Driver" on the license, finds two credit cards, two hundred-dollar bills, and a current picture ID card from the Eidolon Corporation. "At least this nutty fucking chick is gainfully employed," he says aloud to the empty room.

Abby had prepared him for what he'd find in the bathroom. She's prone to exaggeration, but this time she painted him an accurate picture. The way the tile grout absorbed the blood bothers him to the point that he dry heaves. After expending his cache of paper towels and a full bottle of 409, Lawton takes his Hefty bag to the dumpster behind the building.

* * *

Dylan wakes groggy, confused, and naked beneath a hand-knitted afghan covering her from toes to chin. She senses light though her eyes are still closed, and she hears the background static of road traffic in the distance and assorted birds outside. Nausea oscillates in her gut, and her head vibrates in a haze worthy of a car crash. Joints are stiff and muscles sore, as if her organs have fossilized. Hoping to oxygenate her brain back to working order, she breathes deeply, and the smell of window cleaner and oranges fills her nostrils. Despite the pressure in her bladder, she could spit sand, burp dust.

She reaches under the afghan for her hip and scrambles to her feet. Her new wound is bandaged, but she doesn't remember dressing it herself—gauze and white medical tape in place as if a professional bandaged her. Where is the store-bought, rectangular patch?

Making her way to the bathroom, she expects to find the blood-soaked tile floor, but instead, she steps onto an immaculate postage stamp of linoleum surrounding a beige commode. In place of the electric hiss of the motel's lighting, she hears those birds outside, still distant, but gaining in volume. She instinctively holds her breath. She can't even guess how long she's been asleep. As dry as her throat is, it could have been days or even weeks she's been prisoner in this pristine little room. Exiting the bathroom, she surveys the new location, not knowing where she is or how she got there. She feels like an explorer with amnesia.

Three of the four walls have something centered: a window, a painting, the closed door. And instead of the sagging, conjugal bed in the motel, she realizes she awoke on a metal-framed futon against the only bare wall. She exhales to clear her head. She's not supposed to be here. She's supposed to be in her motel room, preparing to go home. She looks down at her naked pelvis, and instead of seeing blood dyed into her skin, she's clean, though she doesn't remember showering. Someone has washed her. Erased all traces. Her skin is white as the bandage.

This small room might be an outbuilding on a forgotten

piece of land in the unincorporated part of town, miles of dusty one-lane road or trail dividing her from the comfort of what she knows as her own—the safety of suburbia, her parcel tucked amid look-alike houses in a semi-gated subdivision on the soccer-mom side of town. Or, this little room could be a cult hideaway. A clubhouse. A back-alley crack house. A private room in some minimum-security rehab for whack jobs. She wants to check the door to see if it's locked from the outside, but is in no mood to know the answer. She swipes a finger over the framed watercolor on the wall, a landscape with two trees rising together before a mountain and purple lake. Dylan can't tell if the painting is priceless or homemade, but the trees hold her attention for a moment. The place is, at least, clean.

The door swings open and a woman walks in. Her arrival at that spot, at that instant, makes Dylan hold her breath, this time in a fighting position, feet wide, hands up, ready to defend herself. When she recognizes the woman, it all comes back to her—Abby.

The sensation of seeing a familiar face is overwhelming for a moment. Pleasure and disbelief cycle through the cavity of Dylan's chest. Even after kicking Abby out last night, here she comes again. For a brief moment she enjoys Abby's presence, but the acid burn of complete insecurity replaces the warm flutter in her stomach as she stands before her naked. Dylan covers her scars as best she can, each hand grasping the opposite shoulder, before deciding to pick up a tin garbage can from beside the bed and cover her pubic area. She covers her nipples with her other forearm. And to avoid further sabotaging herself in front of Abby, Dylan decides to go with her strength of being quiet. Her focus on silence is so encompassing it snuffs away the anger of being displaced against her will.

"Good morning, sexy," Abby says. As she talks, Dylan notices a platinum glow surrounding her head and torso. It takes Dylan a minute to attribute it to the sunlight beaming in from the window. Dylan recognizes Abby's small nose, the squared chin. She appears rested, refreshed. Her brown hair is pulled back from her face in a full ponytail. She carries a carton of orange juice and the memories of the previous night. Abby opens the spout, leans forward, and hands Dylan the juice. Dylan removes her hand from her chest, takes the container, and drinks without speaking.

"I bet you're thirsty. How're you feeling?" Decency feathered with concern. Her voice comes out crisp, clear, and direct. Diction like a high school English teacher. She tilts her head as she speaks. Her brown hair brushes her shoulder, bare and taut, exposed through a white halter.

Dylan feels thin streams of juice flow down the sides of her mouth as she drinks in huge, repetitive gulps, greedy to get it all in.

"Did you sleep, okay? I hope you were comfortable." She tilts her head again.

Dylan adjusts the garbage pail and then pulls away from the juice. "I need some water, too."

Abby's thin eyebrows arch and her smooth forehead turns Shar Pei before she says, "Fuck. Excuse me." She swivels her head and calls through the open door. "Lawton! Could you bring in a bottle of water, please?" Turning back to Dylan, she says, "By the way, you're welcome for the juice."

There's no response from the other room, but someone out there rises with that fart-sound of bare skin on Naugahyde. The noise is something Dylan forever associates as a prelude to pain. Out of instinct, Dylan braces herself when she hears it; a conditioned response like Pavlov's beaten dog. For years, that sound meant her father had sprung to his feet from his cheap recliner so he could smack her or her mother whenever either of them spilled beer or the gravy from a TV dinner or anything else during delivery from the kitchen to his chair. Or for making noise while he slept in front of the Armed Forces television station. Or for having her shirt untucked.

"Where am I?" Dylan says.

Abby tilts her chin, exposing the strong underside of her throat. *Is that a hickey?* Dylan's hickey!

"My house," Abby says.

"Why, exactly?"

"Maybe I'm Kathy Bates and you're James Caan," she says, flexing her right cheek into a half smile.

Dylan stares at her.

Abby reaches out a hand to poke her shoulder. "It's a joke. *Misery.* Old Steven King movie?"

"I get it. It's just not funny."

Abby leans into the doorjamb like a jay landing on a branch outside the window. Even relaxed, she has perfect posture. She smiles and then says, "It's a little funny." She points her bare toes and then squeezes them into foot fists. She holds each contraction for a beat while clicking the nails on her free hand.

"Seriously." Dylan takes a step closer to her. "Why am I here?"

"I couldn't just leave you like that."

"Why the fuck do you care?"

Abby lowers her voice to a whisper. "I think you know."

"Please. I've got no fucking clue." She drinks more juice.

"Let's spare each other the whole fate conversation."

"What?"

"Besides, I couldn't just leave you there for the maid or manager or whoever to find. To freak out. And you were in no position to come up with a better idea, so I threw you in the car and here we are."

Dylan doesn't reply.

"So," Abby says. "You got a little carried away, huh?"

"I don't really talk about it."

"I understand." She reaches out to stroke Dylan's arm with the tips of her fingers.

"I guess you had me a little too worked up."

"That's flattering," she says, still stroking Dylan's arm.

"It was a mistake. I don't normally go that deep."

"Deeper than you realize, sexy," Abby says through a smile. "Deeper than you realize." She turns to face the doorway and pokes her head into the hall.

Dylan can't imagine who might be in the other room, but as long as this Lawton person brings in a bottle of water, she'll be grateful no matter if it's Abby's husband, boyfriend, kid, or even a partner in crime.

Abby hears Lawton whistling in the hall before he appears shirtless in the doorway to the guest room. His torso is more than beach-on-the-weekend tan. It's deeper, leathern—the color of people who live outdoors. He prefers spending his Sundays reading the paper in front of news shows, and she hasn't given him a moment's peace today.

He slings a bare arm over Abby's shoulder. "How's our patient?" Lawton's calloused hand is rough on Abby's skin as he holds out the bottle of water to Dylan with the other, presenting it like a rifle in a soldier's inspection. "Here," he says, twitching his nose in that sinus relieving way both he and their father have.

Dylan doesn't take the water right away. She stays still until Abby notices her gesturing with her eyes. "The cap," Abby says, and twists open the bottle in Lawton's grasp.

Dylan swings her arm away from her breasts and takes it. "Thanks," she mutters, then drinks in a long, slow motion.

"This is Lawton. He's the one dressed your wound," Abby says, patting Lawton's shoulder.

Dylan drains the bottle. "Thanks, again," she says when she comes up for air.

Lawton points in the direction of the bandage. "Just got to keep that dry. It'll be fine."

"Isn't that a perfect bandage?" Abby says, pointing toward Dylan's pelvis, leaning in to pull the garbage can away. With her free hand, she pats the bandage as if to smooth the edges of the tape, but really just using it as an excuse to take a longer, closer look.

Dylan shifts her weight, and readjusts the garbage can. "Are you a doctor? Paramedic?"

"Lawton's in lawn care," Abby says, standing upright.

Lawton extends his hand to shake. Dylan sets the empty water bottle on the bed. She scratches her pubic hair with two quick flicks of her fingers before reaching to grasp Lawton's hand. Respect and disrespect at the same time. Thank you. Fuck you.

"Why is she still naked?" Lawton asks.

"Please tell me you remembered to bring her clothes."

Lawton doesn't respond right away, so Abby punches him in the arm.

"You didn't bring them?" Dylan asks. "What the hell is that?"

"I forgot them in the room."

"Fuck." Dylan plops onto the edge of the bed frame dejected, like a commuter who just missed her train. She reaches for the empty water bottle and squeezes the crinkling plastic. "What the fuck?"

"Don't sweat it." Abby looks at Lawton and winks. "We should have plenty of clothes for you to wear home."

"The sooner, the better," Lawton says to Abby on his way out of the room.

Once he's gone, Dylan shakes her head. "This is just great."

Abby wants to explain herself—wants to lay everything out for Dylan as if an artisan in pursuit of a commission. She's lost dozens of candidates over the past few years and time is running out. And, just like the others, this one is jittery already. Instead, she says, "You've got the biggest lips I've ever seen on a white girl."

"I shouldn't be here," Dylan says. "What are you and your boyfriend up to?"

"My boy...?" Abby laughs and her ponytail swings back and forth as she shakes her head. "You mean my brother, Lawton."

"Your—"

"That's right." She laughs again. "My brother. And for the

record, he's on our side." She looks at Dylan and watches the slightest bit of tension ease out of her bare shoulders. Abby can't help feeling she should have reminded Lawton about the clothes. He had enough to contend with when he went back to clean up the place. "I'll get you back to the motel after you eat something."

Instead of replying, Dylan stares deeply into the garbage can.

"Hey." Abby snaps her fingers in front of Dylan's eyes. "How do you like your eggs?"

Dylan feels overexposed. She holds the shorts and tank top in her hands. They're Lawton's clothes because Abby's are just too small. It's early summer and the warm temperatures make a long sleeve shirt impractical, but a tank top will show too much. Exposing her body and her scars in this house is bad enough, but going out in public like that is something else. "I don't mean to sound ungrateful," she says, "but this isn't going to cover much."

"You'll look great," Abby says.

Without knowing what to say, Dylan slides into the shorts feeling bad she doesn't have underwear, but not bad enough to borrow those, too. The coarse cotton weighs heavily against her bandage, but the shorts are mercifully loose around hips that usually fill out her outfit. Her scarred arms poke through the sleeveless tank top. She slips into the rubber flip-flops Abby loaned her.

Abby turns and leaves the room. "Come eat. You need your strength."

On her way out of the room, Dylan looks around before realizing she has absolutely no belongings there to gather. She follows Abby, empty-handed.

The kitchen is galley style and opens into a family room, where

Lawton lies sprawled backward across an ottoman. Dylan can't tell whether Lawton has fallen or is stretching himself for unknown therapeutic reasons. The Sunday paper is strewn about the room, but he doesn't seem interested in reading it. Dylan takes a seat at the little breakfast bar that divides the kitchen from Lawton and the ottoman in the living room. Along the back wall, floor-to-ceiling bookshelves surround the thick black box of an old projection television, which casts a shadow on a stereo flanked by speakers too large to be new. The oversize TV is off and there's no music playing. She turns to the kitchen. The counter beneath her arms is bare except for three different magazines spread out and opened, as if to the pages someone last read.

Dylan watches Abby turn on one of the stove's gas burners. Her back is to Dylan, and her movements are swift—not fast, but purposeful and with no wasted motion. She cracks an egg into the frying pan with one hand and tosses the shell into the sink four feet away. She cracks and tosses a second, then a third before placing Ezekiel bread into the oven to toast. Dylan is momentarily lost in her motions. The circumstances are all wrong, but she can't help staring. Just hours earlier, she had sex with this woman and now she's cooking food for her. Dylan has never experienced this kind of domestication as an adult.

Abby unsheathes a knife from a wooden block next to the sink. Dylan isn't drawn to sharp objects as a rule, and isn't into knives for anything more than their utility, but the glint of this knife's edge catches her attention with a jolt of electricity up her leg. Abby uses the knife to slice a tomato and Dylan feels another shock.

As if by magic, Abby sets a plate down in front of Dylan stacked with scrambled eggs, two pieces of buttered toast, tomato slices, and what appear to be tater tots, like the ones she got in ninth grade in Norfolk. Abby points with a fork before handing it to her. "Salt and pepper right there."

"This," Dylan says, gesturing to the plate, "is amazing." She looks up in time to see Abby throwing away the frying pan and spatula. "What happened?"

"What do you mean?"

"The pan?" Dylan says, before taking a forkful into her mouth.

"It's old and beat to shit. I'll pick up a new one tomorrow. Now listen, I've got to go change while you eat. I'll set these here, too," Abby says, placing two bananas and another bottle of water in front of Dylan. "I'll be right back."

Dylan nods, another mouthful of egg poised. She chews slowly.

From its perch atop the open trash bag, the nearly spotless nonstick surface of the pan calls to Dylan's sense of thrift and cleanliness, but she resists getting up to wash and dry the perfectly good pan. She isn't used to being a guest in somebody's home, and it isn't her pan.

When she looks up from another bite, Lawton has hopped onto the counter between the sink and refrigerator, directly across from her. Dylan doesn't acknowledge him right away, but when it coincides with slurping in another bite of eggs, she nods toward him.

Lawton doesn't say anything, stares at Dylan.

Dylan wipes her mouth.

The staring goes on for another round of eating and mouth wiping.

Then again.

"I'm sorry to be eating so fast," she says, "but it's been a while."

"You don't have to explain to me."

"This must be pretty weird for you," Dylan says.

"Ordinarily I'd say the same thing to you, but I don't know you. I don't know your deal."

"I assure you—"

"No, you don't," Lawton says, flipping hair out of his eyes with a nod of his head. "You can't assure me of fucking anything because you won't be around long enough. Got that?"

Dylan takes a bite of toast and leans back on the stool. "Excuse me?"

Lawton lowers his voice and says, "Just make sure you get yourself gone as soon and as completely as possible."

Dylan deflects the statement the only way she knows how. "These are the best eggs I've ever had."

"You're no match for her."

Dylan could debate her ability to handle any number of things, but instead she remains silent. Besides Abby, she and Lawton have nothing in common, unless you count their nearly identical clothing. It's a disgrace for Dylan even to be dressed in shorts and a sleeveless shirt. Both of them, it seems to Dylan, are too old to dress that way. However, Lawton is technically her host and Dylan must show nothing but courtesy and appreciation. She's practiced such repression every day at work for hours at a time, so a few minutes with Lawton will be nothing.

"I don't know what you mean," Dylan says, searching Lawton's eyes for the giveaway signs of intent.

Lawton is poker-faced. "She thrives on weakness."

At first, Dylan is insulted and tries to interpret what weakness Lawton might be referring to. She's not gullible enough to believe everything, but she is cynical enough not to disbelieve a fucking thing. "What are you getting at?"

"You're not prepared for her."

Before Dylan can reply, Lawton looks over to the doorway.

Abby's changed from denim shorts and a halter into a severely sensible black business suit. She looks professional in the skirt and matching jacket, but still sexy with bare legs extending into black high-heeled pumps. The suit is not pristine, but it is unfaded, and with the black shoes, she is an exclamation mark. Transformation quick and complete, she's made herself look like a television lawyer in the time it took for Dylan to eat her breakfast.

Lawton's smile is greeted with one of her own. "What's this about?" he asks.

"I've got a thing." She grabs her keys off a hook by the door. "Let's go."

Dylan looks at Lawton, then back to Abby as she points. "What about the dishes?"

"Just leave them."

Outside, Dylan smells the Gulf but can't see it. The sun cuts into her at an angle, suggesting late afternoon. Her skin is pale beneath the revealing clothing she's forced to wear, and the warmth of the sun makes her all the more conscious of her exposure. She does the best she can to cover herself, but she can't get around being so grossly behind schedule. She squints as she makes her way to the passenger side of the car. As soon as she opens her door, the smell of coffee hits her. A dozen empty Starbucks cups litter the back seat, but she's relieved by the absence of blood on the leather seat she finds herself occupying for the second time, although she has no recollection of the first.

"Nice car."

"Please. I've got one more month on the lease and then it's back to the dealer before shit starts falling off of it."

"It looks brand new."

Abby fires up the engine, which purrs to life beneath the shiny hood. "Four years old. I still can't believe I got suckered into such a long lease."

Dylan had bought her Camry used during her second year of college. It has over one hundred thousand miles on it and it's never occurred to her to get a new one. And she's never wanted her old car as badly as she does now. She needs it so she can get home and resume her normal schedule.

As Abby backs out of the driveway, Dylan asks, "Aren't you going to buckle up?"

"Please," Abby says.

"Aren't you going to buckle up?"

"I heard you," she says, looking over at Dylan. "But why would I do that?"

"Safety."

"Safety?" Amazement escapes her lips. "Suddenly, the girl bleeding herself dry and waving razor blades around like free tickets is safety conscious?"

How wrong fucking first impressions can be. "That's not the reason I do it."

Dylan looks away to avoid eye contact, and is treated to the underside of Abby's leg as it lifts from the seat just enough for her to move her foot to the brake. With her thigh back on the black leather seat, she shifts into drive.

"What *is* the reason?"

Dylan sinks her shoulders a little farther back into the seat to alleviate the tension building there. The hot leather on the headrest makes her scalp sweat and she's at a loss. "As a rule," she finally says, "I don't discuss it."

Instead of making an issue of it, Abby says, "I never thought you would."

"They're proven to save lives. Seat belts, I mean."

Abby smiles without taking her eyes off the road. "That's why I don't wear one."

"What's that supposed to mean?"

She smiles and says, "As a rule, I don't discuss it."

The heat radiating off the seat burns through Dylan's baggy shorts, and without underwear, the tender skin along her crack feels singed.

As they drive down streets she doesn't recognize, sunlight refracts through the windshield, illuminating the scars on her thighs. She shifts her hips and hucks down the hems of the shorts. Their naked knees are so close to one another. Her hands are in her lap and her arms are tucked to her body to conceal as much of herself as possible, but there's no way to hide in that sleeveless shirt. With Abby pressed and polished nicer than the VPs in marketing where Dylan works, she feels like a kid being driven to school by a truant officer.

Looking back to the road, Dylan studies their route and estimates that Abby's house is the third point of a triangle that includes as the other two points the motel and the bar where they hooked up. Each point approximately three miles apart.

It's raining by the time they get to the motel. The past week had kept Dylan so excited by the ritual she hadn't paid the weather forecast any attention.

The sight of the motel through the windshield makes Dylan shudder at the thought of the mess left behind the previous night. All the blood. The evidence. The motel didn't appear to be the type of place with a punctual housekeeping staff, so there isn't much fear someone will have discovered and reported the incident, and though she came prepared to deal with the mess, she never anticipated waiting until the following day to clean it up. Everything will be dry, caked on.

"Here we are," Abby says. "The scene of the crime."

Dylan stares at her.

Abby shifts in her seat. "I mean, here we are."

Dylan looks at the motel. In front of her door, their door, sits her Camry. "I guess I'd better get in there and get busy."

"If you mean the mess, it's cool. It's been taken care of."

"What?"

Abby smiles, her lips together. "I sent Lawton down here to take care of it earlier, while you were sleeping. I would have done it myself, but I didn't want to leave you there alone in case you woke up."

Dylan feels something tugging her toward Abby. It's unlike anything she can compare it to directly, and it makes the hair on her arms stick up. In a burst of clarity, she recognizes it as emotion—genuine feeling—and she wants to break free and run in a sort of emotional autotomy, where she abandons her heart the way a gecko sacrifices his tail to escape. She can do this, knowing, like the gecko, she'll grow a new one. It's a survival mechanism, a physiological response to traumatic episodes she endured years ago.

Now, however, she doesn't know what to say. She owes Abby. Is, in fact, grateful to her for all she has done—all the kindness she's extended since catching her. On the other hand, had this woman minded her own fucking business and granted Dylan the privacy she so clearly demanded, she would have been party to none of it. In a sense, she invaded her world, her life, then pretended to be some sort of pseudo Florence Nightingale.

Sitting there, Dylan notices Abby's hair is no longer a ponytail but rather a sophisticated gathering in a broad clip with a black flower. Silent tension wedges them apart, but the confines of her car keep them close.

Abby looks at her watch and bites her lip. "Oh, shit. I've got to go." Her shoulders sink with disappointment and her chin quivers a little and when she hands Dylan the room key, her fingers linger. Dylan doesn't know if she should kiss her or punch her.

"It's not like I want to leave," Abby says.

Outside the car, water sheets off the roofline and slaps the pavement below.

"You've been so generous with your time as it is." Dylan resorts to business acquaintance speak when she's uncomfortable.

Abby leans over, wraps the fingers of one hand around the headrest, and pulls Dylan's face into hers. Her tongue does things in Dylan's mouth that she's never experienced. She chews her lips with her teeth, while alternately licking and sucking her tongue.

Abby releases Dylan, sits back, and looks out the windshield. "Call me later. Or tomorrow."

Excitement races through Dylan's mind. She's off the hook. The famous "call me" line. How perfect is that? This is going to be a clean break after all. "I'll get these clothes back to you after I wash them," she lies.

"No rush. Lawton will never miss them."

When Dylan stands outside the car and bends down to talk through the open door, her back is quickly drenched by the rain. "Okay, then. I'll talk to you soon." Again, she lies.

"You realize that we *will* see each other again soon," Abby says, "don't you?"

Lightning flashes, to the right and then to her left, and thunder cracks *bang-bang* in the space between Dylan and the street. She's soaked and feels a chill on her neck and under her legs as she fingers the key in her hand. "I have every confidence," she lies a third time, shutting the car door.

Three

Bridge traffic is light, even for a Sunday, and Abby speeds through the rain-slick corridors of the Veterans Expressway, hoping to make it in time for the viewing. The funeral, apparently orchestrated for a conventional burial, now requires everyone to have umbrellas instead of sunglasses, and instead of going to the burial, all she needs is to get to the viewing. It isn't like her to be late. She'd allowed Dylan to distract her because every minute she spent with her, the more perfect she revealed herself to be.

A couple of miles from the funeral home, traffic condenses to interior roads, where she finds herself surrounded by luxury cars and all manner of restaurants and banks. People spend some cash on this side of town, though most of them, she suspects, are one flat tire away from missing a payment somewhere.

By the time Abby arrives at the funeral home it's 1:15 and the rain is light enough for her to dash in with only a folded newspaper to cover her hair. Nobody is there to hold the door open, and in her rush to get in, she rakes the corner of the oversize wooden door across her left instep. In the instant that wood gouges leather, brightness flashes in her eyes and pain shoots to her brain. It's the same foot she twisted carrying Dylan. Her throat barely locks down a yelp because it hurts like a bastard, and they have already started the service. The pain makes her think of Dylan. The scars. All that pain—so visible.

With the ceremony started, there is no funeral director stationed by a credenza shaking hands and handing out memorial folders. There is also no crowd Abby can blend in with. She limps her way to the guest register and signs *Beatrice Steele,* because it's the name she uses every time she goes to funerals. As she bends to squeeze her foot, grateful she didn't wear sandals, the folded newspaper falls from beneath her arm. She leaves it there while poking around the stitching of her shoe. The leather is intact. A scuff is better than a gash, in either the shoe or her foot, but there's still a distinct throbbing through the invisible wound. She bites her lip and again thinks of Dylan.

Goodall's Funeral Home is the Neiman Marcus of way stations, all wood paneling and crown molding, chandeliers and wool rugs. It's intimate in a "we care about you" way, with conversation areas and silver-plated tissue boxes on pie tables within reach, but substantial enough to make Abby consider the overhead an operation like this pads into their bills. Most funerals that start here motorcade to Highland Hills, the Martha's Vineyard of final destinations.

Still holding her foot, Abby notices a taste of blood filling her mouth from where she bit it a moment ago, and she can't hold back another brief thought of Dylan.

Abby distributes a portion of her one hundred twenty pounds onto the hurt foot. It's stiff but stable. Inhaling into an upright position, Abby catches the funeral home aroma of carpet and cleaning chemicals for the first time. After walking around on the foot a little, she retrieves her newspaper, takes a prayer card off the credenza, and turns to go in.

As she does, an old man in a black suit and red tie sidles up to her. She bites the inside of her lip again, harder than the last. She doesn't like old people. Can't stand them. They make her nervous. They represent the nature of decay taking its toll on their bodies, their minds. Like the old cars her brother used to work on, with their bad gaskets, blown manifolds, and choked-off carburetors droning noise and sporadic explosions of exhaust. This guy is reason enough to want to die young. He stands there, his orthopedic shoes inches from her black pumps, and she thinks he's likely to make this difficult for her. Of all the funerals she's been to, no one has tried to keep her out.

The old guy has a few gray strands of hair fringing a liver spot plastered on the left side of his skull. Neither of them speaks and Abby wonders if the iron in his eyes is from a lifetime of pain or if it's just part of his job.

He smiles at her. "I'm Vincent's uncle, Cleve Bejeak. And how did you know Vince?"

"I knew him from work," Abby lies, then slips toward the chapel door. But her foot hurts, and movement isn't as quick or as sure as normal. Before making it to the door, the old man reaches for her arm. He's too slow to connect, but the wind of the attempt is enough to turn Abby around, knocking her newspaper and prayer card to the ground.

"Vince was a full-time graduate student," he says, staring at her.

Abby's arm extends, her knees bend, and she holds eye contact with him as she squats in her clamped-knee, tight-skirt way to pick up the paper. The old man is still looking at her, and her organs bottom out, hitting her pelvic floor as she formulates a response. She looks down and sees the prayer card on the floor, like nothing more than a candy wrapper on the street, and decides to leave it there. "I meant from my work."

"Really? Where's that at?"

"The office supply store," she says, hoping he doesn't question it further.

"My nephew was last seen in the company of an unidentified woman. You're an unidentified woman. Identify yourself."

Abby stands, tucks the newspaper under her arm. "My name is Beatrice Steele."

"We heard the unidentified woman was a stripper."

"He never impressed me as the type," Abby says. "Why, do I look like a stripper?"

"You look too classy a woman, if you're asking me. Now if you'll excuse me, I'm on my way to piss again. Huge prostate.

Not that it affects me in other ways, you know," he says with another smile that Abby can't distinguish between passing humor and perversion.

"I'm going in now," Abby says, turning fully.

Taking a seat in the back pew, she counts twenty-eight heads in front of her. Usually the 10:00 a.m. and 3:00 p.m. services draw the bigger crowds, but twenty-eight is nothing to bitch about.

She crosses her legs and notices her spray-on tan is starting to fade and streak. She wishes she'd worn pantyhose. At the podium, the pastor, in a white robe and yellow sash, is reading over the agenda. Abby doesn't have an agenda. Or do they call them programs? She's surprised she doesn't know this detail.

The guy in the box at the front of the room is a guy she tested out a couple of weeks ago. She met him at a coffee shop, where depression read on his face as boldly as the title on the philosophy textbook on the table next to his café latte. She wasted the better part of two months on that poor, sweet, gutless bastard. She'd plied him with sex, and he wasn't bad, really, except for the halitosis and fetish for hand jobs. He'd spent a small fortune on various gloves and lotions and a very expensive rabbit pelt, if for no other reason than to keep his brand of sex interesting for her.

He was a graduate student less than a year away from his Ph.D. Before that, he became a cop to justify not going into the service. He went back to school to justify leaving the police force. Abby thought he'd go with her on schedule, but late last week the guy got a little too anxious and jumped the gun before Abby could explain everything. She isn't going to make that same mistake with a cool prospect like Dylan.

Abby can't get a glimpse of Vince in the casket from where she sits. She also can't help thinking if he'd only waited another hour to shoot himself, she might be in a casket of her own right now. The proximity to his corpse makes the roof of her mouth itch. She forces back anger to absorb sorrow, witness grief.

To her, funerals are the ultimate ending to lives worth remembering, if for no other reason than for their brevity. Funerals for children and old people just don't hold the tragedy of losing someone in their prime like this. With infants to teens, there's always the "what ifs," the speculation of what they might have become. Losing them is sad, but it's just fantasy. No kids turn out how the adults around them envision. And with old people, there are all the memories of a long life. It's nostalgia. Sentimentalism. Abby accepts both for their legitimacy, but the thought of being struck down in that diamond spot, the apex center just after you've become who you are, but before you start changing out of what you've managed to be, is the real tragedy.

Looking down at the obituary in the newspaper in her lap, she sees Vincent Bejeak, a twenty-seven-year-old former cop turned graduate student. The obits never give cause of death, but she knows Vince used the nickel-plated .38 he kept in a shoebox beneath his bed. His permit to carry the thing impressed Abby as his most attractive trait.

Up front, a guy with a large forehead cantilevered by a receding hairline and a braided ponytail delivers the eulogy. He's in khakis and a tattered herringbone jacket too warm for this time of year. And from where Abby sits, sadness reads on the man's pockmarked face.

Abby tugs down the hem of her skirt and further surveys the sea of cotton collars and best-they-could-do hairdos in front of her. In the second row, four men with crew cuts and black blazers cut silhouettes like superheroes. These guys are probably the uncles Vince talked about, the ones who went from the Navy and Marines right into law enforcement. They sit too rigidly to be mourning, and their width blocks the woman crying the most intensely. She's clearly Vince's mother, Helen. The woman pulls tissues out of her purse, but the act of wiping her eyes is blocked between black blazers.

Usually, the gathered are a mix of dry-eyed in-laws, those pretending to weep, and the truly bereaved, all hunched forward and moist, looking like they have the flu. Spouses and parents are the worst. Looking at the backs of these heads, Abby can tell everyone behind the front row is dry-eyed, sitting there doing what they're supposed to.

A pew on the right side holds ten people, but apparently none related to the deceased. A couple are uniformed cops. They're all neutral-faced. Respectful enough, focusing their attention forward, but anyone can tell they've got other things on their minds.

Also in the newspaper folded in her lap, two announcements are circled in red. Vincent's reads, *in lieu of flowers, contributions should be made to the United Way.* It strikes Abby as odd. There are three fifty-dollar arrangements in front of the casket. They look small nestled in between the potted plants the funeral home uses to fill in the space there.

She looks at her watch, wondering how long it will be before she can get close to the casket and curse that bastard for going without her.

The newspaper shows another funeral scheduled for 3:00 over at DuGraw Gardens, a forty-minute drive away. It's a place more specialized in graveside only services, those ten-minute deals better known as McFunerals because they're little more than a drive-through affair. But even these are better than direct burials, which have no ceremony at all. Embarrassed families of AIDS-related deaths usually order those. Unaccepting to the end.

After three prayers and four organ songs between a Bible reading and a moment of silence, the tallest of the crewcut boys in black blazers reads a statement on behalf of the family. As terse as it is, he must have written it himself. His voice has that fear-of-public-speaking shake in it, but there is no hint of sentimentality. He ends it, "No one can imagine how much Helen is going to miss Vincent." Touching. Abby wonders, where is the poetry? Why isn't someone singing "Amazing Grace" a cappella?

Just then, "Amazing Grace" plays from an organ in the corner of the chapel, signaling the service has come to an end. Typical. Abby rises and watches mourners file out trying to look somber, their heads bowed, taking a last look at their Vince-in-the-box.

The viewing must have been before the service. Sometimes everyone stays and mingles, trying not to look at the casket while telling each other stories about the person of honor. Someone is always unsuccessful at stifling a laugh. Now though, everyone has left and it looks like they're going to load the casket into the hearse and go right to the cemetery. But Abby has to get a look at him first. That's half the reason she's there.

As the last guest leaves, she walks down the aisle toward the casket. Casket, not coffin. A year ago, at the Jar Ari Temple while sitting in a wingback chair off to the side, she heard a rabbi tell a little boy in an umbrella of a yarmulke that coffins are actually the old time, six-sided boxes like in old vampire movies and Westerns. "Coffins are wider at the shoulders," he'd said. "Narrow at the feet. Caskets are always rectangles." It's the way he drew the shape in the air with his fingers that made her remember the difference, and the rabbi.

This casket is all black panels and white silk. A few months back, an overzealous funeral associate at Walker & Sons with yellow teeth and burrito breath told her caskets could cost upwards of fifty grand, and this one must be up there. Funerals are all business. Military veterans only go to Arlington if they've been killed in combat, retired, or decorated, and Social Security throws less than five hundred dollars at the deceased's spouse or dependent children, which doesn't dent the expenses. Money isn't really an issue for Abby because her parents have plenty of disposable cash. There will be thousands of flowers at her funeral, which will no doubt look like a coronation.

Despite the open viewing, there's an oil painting of Vince and an eight-by-ten on a table by the casket. Standing beside it, Abby looks in. The corpse there is just that...a corpse. It's not a person. Not anymore. This is not Vince. This is the suspended flesh, bone and organ matter that used to house Vince's soul. Now though, it's hollowed out. Metaphorically speaking, from chemicals flowing through tubes, but if he'd been an organ donor it would be literally, too. Though the notion of donating has a certain magnanimity Abby had realized most strongly the last time she renewed her driver's license, it's not something she could realistically consider. Life to Abby is like leasing a car. It's better to get rid of it before shit starts going wrong. For that reason alone, parting with her liver, her kidneys, or her eyes, though for the greater good of the living, is too much like stripping parts for her to consider. She wants to be missed completely.

They did a decent job on Vince in the back of the house. The face looks good, but the mouth just doesn't look the same. They never do. Before funeral homes display someone, they shave, wash, and dress him. After placing him in the vessel, they close the eyes and mouth—they call this "setting the features." Then they fold the hands at the pelvic region in what they call "an appearance of repose."

She peeks around the head and neck area to see if the embalmer opened the carotid artery too quickly and sucked at the side of his head, denting it like they sometimes do. Embalming takes about two hours. She doesn't know all the ins or the outs, but she's seen where it's done in rooms where porcelain and stainless steel dominate the space beneath fluorescent lights and knows it entails gloves, fluids, needles, and even a scalpel. A two-hundred-pound man like Vincent will have about ten pounds of fluid flushed out of his corpse in the embalming process. It's hard to tell if they stuffed Vincent's suit with towels to make up the difference. He looks good. If she ever sees him in the afterlife, she'll tell him he went out with a pretty good service.

While she's standing there wondering if they used Maybelline or Max Factor foundation to get that color in his complexion, the funeral director comes toward Abby. She's seen this guy a few times. He can't be much older than she is. He's chubby, even under the camouflage of his charcoal, double-breasted suit, and he's got a goatee. Not that she cares, but facial hair seems inappropriate in his line of work. The funeral director meets her halfway between the casket and the family, holding out his hands as if stopping a running child. "Excuse me, Miss—"

"Steele," Vince's old Uncle Cleve Bejeak says from behind them.

The funeral director says to Abby, "The family wants to be alone with Vincent now."

"It's okay, Tom," Uncle Cleve says as he approaches them. "This is Beatrice Steele. She's just here to pay her respects."

Abby gestures with open palm toward the casket. "I just want to pay my respects."

Vince's mother ends her conversation with the preacher and walks toward the group. "Is there something wrong, boys?"

Uncle Cleve stands next to Abby, the button-half of his blazer grazing her ribs. "We're all going to miss Vincent," the old guy says. He then leans into Abby, close enough to smell the garlic on his breath. "He was a shitty cop, but a great nephew," the old guy whispers. He then straightens up and says loud enough for those behind them to hear, "We'll leave you to have some alone time with Vincent."

Abby looks at her watch. Now she has to spend a few minutes there, which will make her late to the three o'clock funeral circled in her newspaper.

Four

As Dylan gets out of her Camry early Monday morning, her white shirt is taut across her chest. She pulls the slack out of the material in the back and checks the tuck around her waist before slipping on her blue suit coat and grabbing the stack of unfinished reports off the seat.

The Eidolon corporate headquarters is in an industrial part of Clearwater on a square-mile campus of concrete, steel, and mirrored glass, where the heat radiates from the asphalt up between the buildings like a smoke stack even at that time of morning.

Early sun sizzles into her back as she walks her daily six hundred forty-two steps across the paved acreage, and the new wound on her pelvis throbs with each step.

Swiping her employee badge over the security device, she wonders if the executives wouldn't rather put the device on the other side of the door, making people prove permission to exit. Like caged animals.

With her arms full, swiping the badge is a challenge that could be avoided if she used the main entrance through the lobby, but doing that requires passing the security station and having to hear the obligatory "G'morning" from James, the midnight-to-eight guy. Dylan would rather crawl three miles on broken glass than exchange pleasantries with strangers like James, especially today.

Walking into the office, hauling her stack of unfinished reports, she's present but not really there. A faxed copy instead of the original document—legible, but blurry at the edges and with lighter text. As she marches past the usual suspects crowded around the coffee station—aimless coworkers unaltered by the events of the past sixty-two hours—she hears them discussing television shows and movies they saw over the weekend. Dylan routinely avoids the banality of pleasantries and the futility of fellowship, but today she pokes her head into the break room. The overweight receptionist stops midsentence in her brag about a double feature on cable Saturday afternoon. "Good morning," Dylan says to her and to the lard-ass from accounting, who stands there listening, sipping from his Big Gulp. They both have donuts in their hands.

"Dylan Rivers," the receptionist says. "We don't see much of you." She has a Diet Coke in her hand and one corner of her lips is up in a smile. She looks nervously at the accountant.

"Well," Dylan says, "you know. Nose to the grindstone and all."

"How was your weekend?" the accountant asks, slurping fluorescent liquid through a clear straw.

"Oh, you know," Dylan says. "Same old, same old." The words are foreign to her, as are the two people in front of her. She's not sure why she struck up this conversation, but fucking with them like this comes with some reward of being out of the ordinary. "But at the end of the day, it's just another Monday. Time to make some money for the man."

The receptionist bites her donut, her eyes darting between the accountant and Dylan.

"Well," Dylan says with as genuine a smile as she can fake, "it's back to the salt mines. Take it easy." She leaves as quickly as she came and doesn't hear any response.

She makes her way to her cubicle, where she removes her suit coat and hangs it over the back of her chair. Before taking her seat, she flips on an electronic fish tank the size of a shoebox sitting on her one cubicle shelf. Her predecessor left it behind years ago and she kept it plugged in. As the fake goldfish bob around, and as if by rote, she dives into her task of portfolio analysis. She writes code and moves data fields to determine if the loan package some broker is trying to sell her company has a high enough percentage of currents. Every loan she analyzes originates at some God-forsaken used car dealership they call Iron Lots where some Buy-Here, Pay-Here huckster inks a contract to finance a car at twenty-four percent for some underemployed sucker who will have to push the dead car before it's paid off. Each morning, Dylan tries to forget about the assholes at the Iron Lots and calculates the par value of each loan.

Today though, it's harder to concentrate on facts and figures. Her mind is on Abby.

Abby.

Abby.

The sensual Samaritan.

But then she hears Winthrop on the opposite side of the partition barricading her from the hallway just outside. The mere sound of his voice makes her nauseous. Bile. She tastes bile. As she hunches forward, her stomach vise grips in a dry spasm and the infinity wound stings beneath the gauze and tape. Winthrop—that figurehead cocksucker—is an animal on Mondays, as if he's been cooped up all weekend and being back at work makes him feel alive, like it's been too long since he's asserted his authority. Winthrop knows little and does less. A waste of space with a doored office. And he doesn't merely speak; he projects everything in a shaky falsetto as garbled and loud as a public address speaker inches from Dylan's ear. Right now he's paraphrasing the mission statement in sound bites, a walking commercial for the company. Out there Winthrop is "team" this and "we" that, but in Dylan's cubicle he curses beneath his breath. His favorite line is, "You fucking slaggard." And from what Dylan's overheard, Winthrop applies the term and the treatment equally to both genders.

The scent of burnt licorice invades her nose as Winthrop's aftershave fills her cubicle. His hair is bushy like steel wool, dyed too dark for his age, and his suit is trendy. He sports deeply set wrinkles, making his face look as if it had been assembled of similar parts, but welded together from the inside. Sweat collects in those channels despite the industrial-strength cooling system.

"Rivers. You're here early again, you hard charger, you." He smiles when he says it, showing teeth the color of old lace, but Dylan knows there's no humor in the comment. "Where's my report?" Winthrop's face flexes as he speaks.

Dylan waves a hand toward the stack of unfinished paperwork on her desk, avoiding eye contact. She just can't deal today.

She's lost count as to how many years ago she last saw Winthrop as a person. Maybe back when she had two mugs that said "One Year of Service" sitting beside that fake fish tank on the lone shelf in her cubicle, while she progressed toward a third. Winthrop was hired from some state job at an engineering research center and ended up as Dylan's boss. The job should have been Dylan's, but back then she just hoped the new guy kept himself half as invisible as the boss who'd just retired. And Winthrop flashed a smile the first week, so Dylan thought her chances looked good. But by the middle of the second, yelling and negativity streamed from his office loud enough to spread fear amongst employees. A receptionist developed a twitch. Things went downhill from there.

Today is the first time Dylan doesn't have a five-page report bound in a three-ring with the company logo printed in fake gold on black plastic to present to him. She has nothing. And for the first time, she fears Winthrop's term "slaggard" might actually apply to her.

Winthrop is more a product of being senior than of having seniority. His age proved significant to the powers-that-be, as if age is indicative of leadership ability.

This is the same guy who gives Dylan "excellent" across the board on her semi-annual evaluations—all the way to the category related to behavior—and then heavy-hands a checkmark in the "needs improvement" column. The first couple times he did this,

Dylan tried to contest the low marks, but Winthrop said, "The more you question it, the more you prove the point." By the third time, Winthrop got careless, or honest, and said, "There isn't anything *truly* unacceptable about anything you do, Rivers, but there's something about the way you hold your jaw, as if everything I say is wrong. It's disrespectful. And bordering on insubordination."

Ordinarily, Dylan keeps chunks of rage docile by going back to the scars. It's automatic. That same Pavlovian response to the trigger of emotion.

"What the hell is this?" Winthrop's question could as easily refer to a turd on the floor as the missing report.

Dylan rolls her eyes. Winthrop's sagging neck bears the bumpy rash left by a dull razor. The way Winthrop's white skin dangles around his jowls, showing spots of red, reminds Dylan of the old white towels her father left hanging in the bathroom—yellowed with age and stained with blood.

"Sorry, boss. I just didn't get through it this weekend." It's the first time she's said those words.

"Well, I have a meeting with the board on Wednesday, so I'll need those reports. Doublecheck the figures accounting sent down. I don't want to stand before the board with my dick in my hands."

Dylan grinds her teeth, creating heat in her mouth until she bites a chunk out of the inside of her cheek. She wonders how many times the asshole will use the word "board." The company's bottom line improved shortly after they both got there, and as far as the board of directors is concerned, they're a team and their status isn't about to change. But no matter how hard she busts her ass, her employee rating is too low to qualify for raises or promotions. Dylan would strangle the son of a bitch, if not for the three daughters in the picture on Winthrop's desk, each girl presumably in or near college.

Before leaving Dylan's cube, Winthrop sees her as if for the first time that morning. He points and says, "Jesus. What the hell happened to you? You look like shit."

"Nothing. Why?" Dylan tucks her shirt further into the back of her waistband.

Winthrop caresses his ass of a chin, studying her. "You look sick. What's your malady?" He allows no time for a reply. "We have no time for delays, so heal yourself quick."

"Oh, sure. Chicken soup ought to clear me right up."

"Whatever." Winthrop turns to leave. "Just don't call in sick. I can't afford having you out for even for one day, you hard charger, you."

Dylan wants to kick his legs out from under him, just to watch him fall. Busybody son of a bitch. Winthrop leaves, no doubt going to niggle the piss out of somebody else.

When noon rolls around, Dylan's stomach is too balled up to accept food. She rolls herself away from the computer with a plan of relieving herself and checking the new bandage to make sure she isn't bleeding through. Though she's a veteran of the ritual, experienced with the process and results, she cut a little deeper that night and would, naturally, bleed a little longer, a little stronger. She might need to reinforce the bandage with toilet paper and more tape. Before she can get up, she hears a knock on the outside of her cubicle wall.

With the exception of Benny Sloat in a cubicle across the aisle from her, almost no one speaks to her. She doesn't need to collaborate with anyone, and the attractive older man's assistance is only for rare occasions when he has to verify offshore acquisitions. Other than him, there isn't anyone she has any type of relationship with, so there are few interruptions...besides Winthrop.

Dylan sees movement in her peripheral vision. A face peering around the cubicle doorway.

"Knock, knock."

"Abby!" Dylan says, rolling further back in her chair. Feeling as if all the air has been forced from her lungs, she inhales as she pushes herself to stand. With her breath comes the scents of spearmint and vodka, and they make Dylan remember Abby naked and the way she felt beneath and atop her.

"Hiya, sexy," Abby says. She places a large paper bag on Dylan's desk and attaches herself to her, one arm around Dylan's neck, the other firmly gripping her crotch. She presses her mouth to Dylan's, but instead of kissing her back, Dylan pulls away. "How did you get in here?"

Abby squints for a moment and says, "What's his name? At the front desk? He's a sweetie. He told me where to find you. I brought lunch." Dylan recognizes the Outback logo on the bag from occasional curbside takeout. The bag contains two Styrofoam to-go containers.

"Lunch?"

"Midday food. Surely you've heard of it."

The fact is, Dylan never takes lunch. On occasion she'll eat a sandwich at her desk, but she never leaves her cubicle for anything longer than a bathroom break. Besides, Winthrop could come around the corner any minute. "I'm awfully busy."

"You've got to eat."

"My boss might walk by."

"I'd like to meet him."

"How'd you know where I work?"

"You mentioned it over breakfast yesterday."

Dylan didn't stop to remember if she did or didn't mention it. "It was nice of you to drop by, but I really must get back to work."

"Fuck that. You need to eat. You're malnourished."

"I'm fine, and I don't have time for it."

"Well, you'll just have to make time," Abby says, setting out plastic knives and forks on large paper napkins. "Do you prefer baked or sweet?"

"What?"

"Your potato. I got one of each. Which do you like better?"

Dylan's too stunned to speak for a moment. No one has ever offered her the choice before. After a moment or two of silence, Abby looks over her shoulder. "Which one?"

"It doesn't matter."

"Oh, but it does matter, Dylan." She reaches out to touch Dylan's chin. "What you want matters to me. More than you know."

Dylan is equally annoyed and flattered. No one has ever taken the time to surprise her so pleasantly. But still. She isn't comfortable with Abby's presence there. "Well, I suppose since you took the trouble to bring it and all."

As Dylan watches Abby, she wonders if this unexpected force of nature might be just what she needs at this stage in her life. But she still isn't sure how to play Abby. Dylan knows Abby isn't the right woman to trust, but at the same time she doesn't care. Abby isn't perfect, but her timing is. Dylan decides right then that she's been concentrating on the wrong aspects of life for too long.

As she chews her first dense bite of steak, Abby opens a large leather bag and removes a bottle of red wine.

"You can't open that here."

"Why not?"

"I don't think it's legal."

"Legal? Please. It would be a crime to eat these steaks without red wine." She pops the cork. "I hope you like medium-rare. Though it's probably medium by now."

Halfway through the meal, Winthrop walks back in. "Rivers," he says, without looking up. "I've got new data I want you..."

Dylan scoots back in her seat, like a dog finding the back corner of his cage. She wants to hide the food and make Abby disappear, but before she can move, Abby speaks.

"Edison Winthrop. I'll be damned. Didn't know you left Kriston and Sons."

All tension in Winthrop's face eases and, for the first time, he displays a semblance of happiness. "Abigail. My God, it's been years. What are you doing here? I mean, pleasant as the surprise is."

Despite the happiness, he speaks the same sycophant routine he pulls with board members and the CEO and Dylan is surprised to see it now.

"I brought my girlfriend a picnic lunch," Abby says.

Dylan recoils at the word "girlfriend," though it's more unexpected than unpleasant.

"You know each other?" Dylan says.

"Yes, yes," Winthrop says. "Of course. I had regular contact with her father's company in my last job."

"Your father's company?" Dylan says to Abby.

"Stratton Industries. A very wonderful company. Abigail is vice president of marketing," Winthrop says.

"Was."

"Was? Really? So what is your title now, Abigail?"

"Vice president of marketing?" Dylan says.

Abby looks over at Dylan and shakes her head. "After college, my father made me take the position. He had me convinced it was what I wanted."

They both ignore Winthrop, which Dylan finds surprisingly easy.

"Well, it was lovely seeing you again, Edison, but our steaks are getting cold."

Winthrop clears his throat. "Ah. Right. Well, then. Carry on. It was good seeing you again, Abigail. Be sure to give my best to your parents."

Once Winthrop leaves, Dylan has a dozen questions ready to go, but holds them in as if they are one big breath. If Winthrop noticed the wine, he sure didn't say anything about it.

A moment later, as Abby's opening a Styrofoam container housing a large Caesar salad, Winthrop reappears. "Just one more question, Abigail, if I may."

Dylan fears the old bastard is going to say something about the wine, though she hasn't touched a drop of the glass Abby poured for her.

"What is it, Edison?" Abby says.

"Did you say Rivers is your girlfriend?"

"That's right."

"Now why on God's green earth would a woman of your caliber want to associate with an animatron like Rivers?"

"You'd be surprised by what Dylan does to please a lady," Abby replies, then takes a huge bite of salad. "Now run along and let us eat," she adds, chewing her mouthful.

On Wednesday afternoon, Abby drives across the bay on I-275 and limps into the L-shaped dressing room at Rifley's Eden dragging a tan leather duffle bag behind her. The area just above the flip-flop on her right foot has swelled into a stout cankle that throbs slow and steady. She used to heal much faster from little injuries like these, but with less than three weeks before turning thirty, she can't expect miracles. The ankle will stay sore. It doesn't matter though because pretty soon she'll be free of pain—free from her body. In the meantime, she'll work.

It's been two days since she's seen Dylan and she has a jones going. When she's in this kind of mood, she needs to hear applause, hoots and hollers, injury or no injury. In the dressing room, Daphne is already there and sitting naked on the denim-covered love seat against the far wall. She's got a plastic bag and needles in her lap and she's staring at them intently. Abby doesn't know how long she's been at her little hobby, but from what she can tell, Daphne's needlework is getting a hell of a lot more professional.

She looks up at Abby and shakes long black hair from her face as she sets the plastic bag of yarn on the floor at her feet. "Born to Ride" is tattooed in red within sprawled angel's wings across her lower back. "Knitting this blanket for a friend's baby," she says, knotting her hair in back and sliding the knitting needles through to hold it up, geisha style.

Star is sitting in a chair, her bare feet propped up on the makeup table, flipping through a copy of *In Touch*. She doesn't look up. Her blond hair is plumped with volume, she's in her cheerleader costume, and she's pretending she doesn't see Abby. Abby sets her duffle bag on a blank space of Formica in front of the mirrored wall. Star flips a page in her magazine. "I didn't see your ass on the schedule."

Raven pokes her head out of the bathroom and leans an arm completely sleeved with tattoos depicting Poe's famous poem on the jamb. She says, "Oh hey, Cassandra," because they only use stage names in the building. They all know her real name, but none of them knows who she *really* is, and she often wonders how shocked they will be when they find out.

"What brings you in?" Raven says, before returning to the bathroom.

"I'm just trying to cover the cost of the party we're having on Saturday. You guys'll be there, right?"

"I've got double shift," Daphne says. "Is it going all night again?"

"Until the last one leaves," Abby says.

"Then I'll be there, eventually."

"Me too," Raven says.

Abby sorts through her duffle bag and removes three packs of false eyelashes, two tubes of Duo adhesive, a large tub of body glitter, makeup, nail polish, her short black wig, wire wig brush, comb, tape, Dermablend body concealer, her short-shorts, cowboy boots, and the plaid shirt she plans to wear as a costume tonight. Then she finds the list she folded twice. She wants to look it over, but decides against it and slips it back into her bag.

Over the magazine, Star says, "Is your new piece of ass going to be there or was that another fuck and forget?"

"What's wrong with you?"

"You fucking ditched us the other night."

"I didn't ditch you," Abby says, unbuttoning her shirt.

The idea is laughable, but Abby holds it in. She's long sought that rare breed of unconditional love paired with a disdain for life. And now, it seems Dylan might actually possess those polar opposite traits. If she had the luxury of time, she could go on with her for a while and see if she develops properly, but the calendar is against her.

Daphne removes the knitting needles and lays them in her lap. Her eyes focus up at Abby. "Have you heard from her since Saturday?"

"I had lunch with her the other day."

"Figures," Star says.

"You have no idea." She can't blame Star for being mad. She did ditch her and the girls Saturday night. "C'mon. I found a hot date. You would have done the same."

"I saw her. She wasn't that hot."

"You have no idea."

"What? Rich?"

"Not in the way you mean it."

"Woman of your dreams, you mean?"

"She just might be."

"Well, we still ain't cool. I'm still mad at you."

"Don't be."

"Then get my back," Star says.

"What?" Abby asks, knowing the answer. "A favor?"

Star grabs Abby's hand, kisses her fingertips. "Work Zoe's Wednesday night shift." She looks up and bats her false lashes.

Abby doesn't pull away, but says, "Why would I do that?"

"Come on, Abby. You're the only one who can make your own schedule. Do it for me."

"What's in it for me?"

"She has to go visit her sick aunt. You'd be helping her and shit."

Abby takes this opportunity to pull her hand away from Star's lips. "I don't care about her or her sick aunt."

"Okay," Star says. "Here's the deal. Straight up, right? Zoe will work for me Saturday if someone works for her next Wednesday. I can't do it. I'm already on that night."

"Saturday night?"

"Damn, girl. I'm mad as shit, but I still want to go to your party. Come on. You owe me." Star winks at Abby and holds out her arms in anticipation of a hug, pouting her lower lip for all it has.

"Fine. Fuck. I'll work next Wednesday night. Whatever." She goes in for the hug. "You're not mad now, right?"

"We'll see how the party goes," Star says, and laughs as they hug.

Raven clomps out of the bathroom in her trademark platform thigh-highs. "Well, is there a chance this hot new girl might show up?"

"Here?" Abby says.

"The party," the women all say, not quite simultaneously.

Abby reaches out, drapes an arm over Raven's shoulder and says, "I'm planning on it."

"Were you limping just now?" Daphne asks.

"I've got to wrap my ankle," Abby says. "It'll be fine as soon as I'm on stage."

After repainting the chipped polish on her fake fingernails from an old bottle of black cherry, Abby stands naked in front of the mirror covering her legs with flesh-colored powder. She dabs the puff into the powder and smooths a liberal amount over her rear. She does this on the insecure or dark days when she's feeling less than perfect. Before going further, she sets the powder down, grabs a towel, and dries the moist areas again before bending over and powdering between her legs, back to front between her thighs.

She needs help to get the center of her back. She can't decide which girl to disturb for the task, and while she waits for a decision to hit her, Kal Rifley, Jr. walks in.

Kal is a pot-bellied man. He wears designer blue jeans and a floral print shirt, tucked in, thousand-dollar shoes, ten-thousand-dollar watch. He's all of twenty-six and inherited the club from his father. Despite his faults, he generally made it hard to dislike him by being sweet and sort of awkward around Abby.

"Need any help, Cassandra?" he says, staring at Abby's back before getting a cheap shot of her front reflecting in the mirror.

"No."

"Well," he says, slicking strands of hair behind his ears, "I'm glad you're here, but don't forget to clock in if you want to make bonus for the day."

She never met old man Rifley, but she heard from the other girls that he would bust balls. This Rifley allowed her to be her own boss. Commissions from what she earned dancing were pure profit, and he would bump any girl from the rotation to satisfy any appearance Abby wished to make. In the beginning, he told her, "If it was up to me, I'd have you here seven nights a week. But I know you've got a life." He never asked questions, and he always kept her spot open at the makeup mirror.

A second after he exits the dressing room, Abby hears the music fire up on the other side of the dressing room wall. It's some techno tune she's heard a thousand times. No doubt the doors have been opened and men are already filing in.

She pulls on her Bettie Page black wig and wedges a straw cowboy hat over it. After wrapping her ankle with the Ace bandage, she slips into little red cowboy boots.

"Cassandra and Daphne to pole five. Cassandra, pole five. Daphne, on deck."

Daphne has a towel wrapped around her waist and it doesn't slip as she bends forward to stretch her hamstrings from atop the pair of seven-inch black lace-ups she wears every day. After stretching, she comes up and checks her long red hair in the mirror.

Outfits and wigs are good for business, but Daphne wears as

little as possible. If it isn't the towel, it's a sheet, or strategically placed whipped cream, but always the same hair and same shoes. It's hard for Abby to believe she is the same Linda who usually wears jeans, old-school tennis shoes, and chandelier earrings.

Abby looks around the room. The girls are all younger, which makes her upcoming birthday even harder to face. She feels old and unprepared today. She stops to dig through the costume and prop swap box in the dressing room, finds a noose left over from Morticia's late night act, and unravels it to use as a lariat. As she and Daphne go through the door to the stage, she uncoils the rope, and in the process, flips her internal switch and is now ready to entertain.

While up on stage with the glare of spotlights surrounding her, the hoots and hollers come out of a faceless crowd like waves from a foggy sea. The sensations invigorate and motivate her to perform a little better than last time. The floor is slick beneath her cowboy boots, but the brass pole between her thighs as she hangs upside down isn't so cold once she begins tugging on her nipples and the crowd roars. Her ankle is suddenly painless. Each performance gets her wetter than the last, and she knows she'll miss it when she leaves.

Five

The following Saturday morning, Dylan works from home. Her computer screen here is bigger than the one she has at work, but the best benefit is that she can take a break and squeeze in one of her workouts without losing much time and without having to speak to anyone.

Constant social interaction came with the territory of working for a corporation, and even while being a Marine. But since her discharge, Dylan avoids crowds or groups. She's never been inclined to join a gym or attend classes at a local martial arts place to spar on a regular basis. Instead, she keeps her skills sharp and herself in shape through conditioning exercises and hand-to-hand combat drills in a room she converted to a home gym.

In addition to weights, a treadmill, a stationary bike, and her yoga mat, she has a heavy bag filled with a hundred pounds of sand that absorbs each punch with just enough give to prevent damage to her hands and wrists. The repeated impact toughens up the bones in both. Each punch rattles the chain attached to an eyebolt in the ceiling. It's anchored to a four-inch oak post secured across the trusses. She did the work herself the first night she'd moved in. The only way that bag might fall is if the whole roof caved in.

A pair of Everlast heavy bag gloves protects her knuckles. Wrist wraps allow her to absorb the impact of each strike. She punches the bag as hard as she can. She throws knees and kicks and elbows from both sides. In between an imaginary round, she drops to the push-up position and pumps out a set of twenty. She's back on her feet for just a moment before she starts another round on the heavy bag.

She's in full motion as she ends her round and hits the floor again. Instead of regular push-ups, or even going from her knees, she challenges herself to press up forcefully enough to clap her gloved hands and return them to the floor in time to catch herself and follow with nine more repetitions.

Her body heat rises despite wearing only boy shorts and a sports bra, the elastic of which cuts into her armpits and will leave a pink line atop her ribcage for hours after removing it. Sweat drips into her eyes and blurs her vision, not just because it's sweat, but because she has oily skin and the salt-oil combination stings. She pauses a push-up at the top and makes herself a tripod as she swipes at the sweat with the back of her glove, like a cat cleaning its face. The air conditioner kicks on, and as soon as the register rattles, the coldness of the forced air chills her skin, makes her aware of the bacteria under her arms. She continues her workout with diamond push-ups, feeling the braided carpet fibers tickle her nose in the bottom position.

The next round on the heavy bag, she pounds the left high kick over and again to make it stronger. Doing so torques her knee. It feels sore. She can't tell if it's swollen unless she stands in front of a mirror, but it doesn't really matter. She knows enough to back it down before she aggravates the knee enough to require discontinuing her training for a week or two. She doesn't want to back off today, but she really doesn't want to miss extended training time. She's learned this as she's gotten older. Perhaps it's the wisdom of age. Perhaps it's just resigning herself to the fact she doesn't recover or heal as quickly as she used to. She scales back on the kicks, focuses on her striking.

The taste of minerals in her tap water makes her drink faster as she replenishes the fluids she's perspired. Instead of finishing with thirty minutes of intervals on the bike and wrapping it up with a five-mile jog on the treadmill, she drops to the floor to begin an intense series of abdominal exercises, which makes her new wound bleed in just the right way.

After a shower, Dylan hears the rubbery, triple gong of her doorbell. She stands, looks at the clock: 10:17. Her instinct is to hide, to pretend she's not home. In that brief instant, she theorizes it might be Winthrop coming to deliver another pile of work. To dump on her another load of "high-priority material" or some such shit. He's done it on numerous occasions. That old fuck has no regard for personal space or privacy.

Dylan then thinks maybe it's a Jehovah's Witness. She hates solicitors, especially those peddling religion at her door. The bell rings again.

She peeks through the pleated curtain hanging over the sidelight by the door. The thermostat is still kicked down to sixty-eight degrees, her sleeping weather, and the chilled inside air meets the sunshine on the other side of the window with a handshake of condensation. She can't see clearly through the sweat on the outside of the windows, but she does see a blurred figure acknowledging her own.

Instead of a clean-cut guy in black pants, white short-sleeved shirt and tie, the solicitor at the door is a four-foot-tall chubby kid wearing a ball cap and a phony smile.

"Good morning, ma'am," the kid says. "My name is Billy Dinkle. My friends call me Dinky." He tips his hat and heaves his fleshy cheeks into an even broader smile. "It's a play on words." The kid stops for a practiced beat, then continues. "I live here in Wakeville Estates and I'm selling raffle tickets for the county Little League. How many would you like to buy today?"

Seeing the Little Leaguer on her front stoop reminds Dylan of herself at eleven years old: chubby, eager, and optimistic. Must be the team catcher. Fat kids always end up as catchers.

"They're a dollar each, ma'am. And you could win a seventy-two-inch flat-screen television, courtesy of Hudson Electronics."

The kid knows how to sell. This efficient pitch must work on normal people.

Before Dylan's old man got stationed overseas, they'd lived in Norfolk, where Dylan became the first girl to play Little League baseball in Tidewater. The league once had a raffle to raise money for a new press box, but her father had forbidden her to participate. "No kid of mine is going door to door like some type of friggin' beggar," the old man said.

"Does your father attend your games?" Dylan asks the kid at the door.

The kid removes his cap and wipes sweat with a plump forearm. "He's assistant coach."

"Must be nice," Dylan says, looking at the kid's new ball cap, pristine except for a sweat stain inching out onto the curved bill.

"So how many tickets can the county Little League count you in for, ma'am?" The kid's pudgy fingers are wrapped around a small stack of tickets, and he waves them like a salesman.

Over the boy's shoulder, Dylan's neighbor across the street, Mr. Wilson, is raking his front yard, though there are no leaves. Wilson always rakes his front lawn for three hours on Saturday mornings, combing the lawn like hair, in little sections.

The kid waves a hand across the street and says, "Mr. Wilson over there bought five. Would you care to match his contribution? Give yourself equal odds of winning?"

Dylan opens the door wider for a moment, looking at the kid, then slowly shuts it, saying, "Stay there. I'll be right back."

Taking her time, she walks to her desk and pulls out the checkbook. It's one of those oversize, commercial-style checkbooks with three checks and matching receipts on each page. She writes out the check, her penmanship as articulate as an architect's, and tears along the perforated line before returning to the front door.

"Here you go," she says, handing the kid the check.

"Holy shit," the kid says. "Are you kidding? I don't have a thousand tickets to give you."

"I don't want any raffle tickets."

The kid leans in, his round face a sponge of urgency. "But you'd probably win."

Dylan shakes her head in a controlled pattern. "I don't watch a lot of television."

"Huh?" The kid looks up from the check.

"Listen, just don't let your pitcher get any balls by you."

"How'd you know I was a catcher?"

Dylan closes the door without answering. Her past is none of the kid's business.

By two o'clock that afternoon, with nothing but the sound of the road beneath her tires, Dylan drives with her left elbow out the open window along what she thinks is Abby's street. The food smells increase in intensity as the economic makeup of the neighborhood shifts down. Small houses and dilapidated duplexes line the street. Only a handful of yards are kept up beyond junkyard status, but each has a satellite dish and a late model car in the driveway or yard. The radio is off and she focuses her concentration. She smells not only garlic and cookies, but also the Gulf's salt water.

Toward the far end of the street, she recognizes what she thinks is Abby's house. She mapped her destination online in advance and she's followed those directions to the letter, but still, she can't be sure if this is Abby's house. Last time, she saw it from a rearview mirror, and now there are cars out front and people crowding the yard so it's hard to be sure. What had been a quiet yard is now filled with parked cars and people milling about, talking in groups, and apparently dancing. Still, Dylan's convinced this is Abby's house. Backing up to park at the end of a long row of cars, she figures the best thing is to scope it out from a distance.

The sun illuminates the people in the yard as colorfully as one of those LeRoy Neiman paintings she saw as a kid; but instead of sports, these people are sharing cigarettes and drinks. A guy in baggy jeans climbs onto the hood of a German car and does a backflip, landing squarely on his feet. Another guy climbs onto the car the same way but slithers back down as a heavyset woman comes from the back of the house. Amongst the crowd Dylan spots Abby, like Joan of Arc surrounded by the English. In that mixed crowd, she is peerless. Her brown hair is down, and her denim shorts and halter are similar to what she wore the morning Dylan woke here.

She watches Abby talk to some faceless grunt with a shaved head and a sleeveless shirt and Dylan's agitation manifests like a convulsion. Every muscle tenses in her now sweaty body, and within moments, her mouth burns from the friction of grinding her teeth.

The tension and flexion hold until Abby breaks away, but before Dylan can relax completely, Abby hugs a big blonde surfer type, then makes her way over to a small group of people where she hugs two girls in low jeans and a skinny guy with dreadlocks past his shoulders.

Abby holds the long neck of a beer bottle loosely between her fingers as she circulates. Neighbors pass from their houses into hers and some do the reverse. Laughing. Touching. Handshakes, hugs and kisses. Everyone holds a drink.

Lawton comes out the front door wearing a Hawaiian shirt, clutching a red plastic cup in one hand. With the other, he snatches off a woman's bikini top in one long pull of the bow. The topless woman stands, hands on her hips, shaking her head, but then chases Lawton around the house and into the backyard. Everyone, including her, laughs.

Dylan redirects her attention back to Abby. She stands in the yard, a hand cupped over her brow like a hiker checking a path in the distance. She's staring right at Dylan. Suddenly, she's waving and is no longer a hiker, but a castaway spotting a plane.

Dylan wants to take off like a thief leaving a robbery. But what has she stolen? She snuck in and grabbed a glimpse of the good life. Not that mythical, country club, ball gown, caviar and crystal kind of good life, but the happy, partying, good friend and neighbor kind of good life—a life she's never experienced before. Still, just a glimpse or not, she is stealing. If she burned the tires smooth to get the hell out of there, would Abby be pissed she left? Would she get in her car and chase her?

She doesn't take off. She's a wax figure of herself and Abby is waving to her as she strides purposefully toward Dylan's car. Before Dylan can react, Abby's leaning into the opened window.

"I was beginning to think you wouldn't make it," she says. "Get your ass in here." She leans in more. For what? A kiss?

Dylan tucks her chin, swipes imaginary lint from her khakis. "I don't know why I came."

"Come meet everybody," Abby says, pulling the car door open. Before she can reply, Abby grabs Dylan's hand and leads her across the street toward the house.

Immediately, the old churning sensation starts in Dylan's stomach and beads of sweat form on her forehead and scalp. She should refuse, but she needs to be near Abby right now. Dylan says, "Why don't we go for a ride?" Abby walks too fast to hear and separation from her is not an option.

They pass uneventfully through the couple dozen people in the front yard and driveway, but inside she finds herself in the center of dozens more people, which gives her a sensation of falling. Crowds are something she avoids to the point of shopping for perishables only twice a month, late on Tuesday nights, and she has dry goods delivered through an online account.

She recognizes the inside of the house, but now the dining room table is covered with liquor bottles and the living room furniture is askew with people dancing. All manner of abandoned drinks sweat on various horizontal surfaces. Dirty shoes trample the carpet.

Dylan's introduced to three tall women, two pro wrestler guys, a personal trainer, a queen with a little dog in a man purse, and an overly happy guy named Awesome Sanchez who seems to be hearing impaired. Dylan's head is falling in concentric circles and she's unable to absorb much of what these people say, but she shakes hands and nods. She feels off balance. The more people come in the front door, the less she wants to be there. The smell of menthol in the air does nothing for her lightheadedness, and the ceaseless techno music thumps into her brain.

Abby grabs her by the shoulder. "This is Terrance," she yells at pointblank range.

"It's good to put a face with the name," Terrance, a skyscraper of a man, says.

Dylan stares up at him. "What?"

While enveloping Dylan's hand with his own, the skyscraper says, "I've heard things."

Over the thump of the chest-pounding techno music, Dylan hollers into Abby's ear, "Walk me out!"

Two more women, who arrive squealing and bouncing, interrupt Abby's attention. They jump around in a hug circle. Then, Lawton, on the other side of the room, thrusts his hand in the air, waving it above the crowd. He hollers something Dylan can't make out as he slithers through the mass of people. The recognition of another face eases Dylan for a moment, until she realizes this is the last person she wants to see.

When Dylan turns to get Abby's attention, she feels hands clasp down on her shoulders again. "Hey, look," Lawton says. "It's the cutter. How you doing, cutter?"

Sweat streams from Dylan's scalp. "Shut up," she mumbles. "Shut your fucking mouth."

Lawton either hears her or thinks twice about making a scene. Instead, he sort of hugs Dylan and uses the close proximity to speak into her ear. "Thought I made myself clear the other day. I don't want you around my sister."

Dylan doesn't try to pull away. No good could come from turning this into a spectacle. Lawton pulls her closer as if they were hugging. It's aggressive, but not foundationally strong. Dylan could escape and reverse the hold instantly if she chose to.

"I'm not as drunk as I look," Lawton says. "Nor am I as nice as you may have been led to believe. You seem like a decent enough gal. You go ahead and enjoy this party, but if I see you near Abby again, I will shoot you twice in the head with the Glock I keep beneath the seat in my truck. And then I'll have that big guy in the kitchen dispose of your body in a remote piece of swampland east of the interstate. Now is that completely clear?"

Before Dylan has time to respond, Lawton hollers, "Okay, babe. Glad you could make it." And then in one swaggering motion, he spins and walks off with a tree of a woman in orange shorts and a canopy of breezy red hair.

As Abby rejoins Dylan, she says, "You'll have to excuse Lawton. He's surprised to see you. Well, surprised and on the wobbly end of a fifth of tequila."

Abby then returns to the group of girls, and this gives Dylan time to look around the room—to witness the party like the perennial fly on the wall that she is. Tiny. Insignificant. A nuisance.

An assortment of crushed cigarette butts is on the tile in the kitchen, where two naked women stand, holding yet more liquor bottles. The latter commands all of Dylan's attention. She fixates on the blond woman, whose hair cascades to the radical curve of her low back, right where her ass begins. Her hips are narrow, but from the side her ass bubbles out and she lacks any tan lines. It's Abby's opposite ass—not better, just opposite—and Dylan's unable to look away.

Another naked woman, this one with long black hair and an arm covered with tattoos, is reclined on the counter serving shots of tequila, apparently, out of her navel—a long and animated line of both men and women wait their turn like jackals at a watering hole. The louder people get, the faster and lower she pours. It's simultaneously erotic and unsanitary. It's like the Playboy mansion in there, but Dylan wishes she could be home watching all these hot women on television instead of being mixed in the crowd with them.

"Yo, chick," the naked blonde hollers from the kitchen loudly enough for Dylan to look away. Dylan tries to slip through the crowd to rejoin Abby, but before she can get away, the woman grabs her wrist. "Hey, you're Cassandra's—I mean Abby's—friend, aren't you?"

"I'm here with Abby, if that's what you mean." Dylan speaks directly to naked tits and immediately regrets it. She looks at her face and repeats her words.

"Well then you need some special greeting," she says, pulling her. "Get in here. Hey, y'all, this here is—" She turns to Dylan. "What's your name?"

"Dylan."

"Yo, this here's Dylan." She sweeps a pointed finger around the small room. "This is my Party Posse. Now let's hook her ass up!"

The next thing she knows, Dylan has her face buried in the reclined brunette's navel and is slurping what she can only imagine is tequila. She's never had liquor before. Naturally unused to the effect, she's immediately intoxicated by the naked woman, if not the booze. She stands up with her mouth full and swallows. The crowd chants, "More. More. More." Dylan gives the thumbs up and bends for another taste. The chanting and collective cheers continues between each of her five belly shots. She wants to grab this woman's torso and splash her down to her shaved pubis and lick until she's dry and then get out her blade. But it's fifty-one weeks too soon. She has to stop.

"Really? You started the party without me," Abby says, as she enters the kitchen. "Thanks for hooking her up, Raven and Star, but we got to mingle now."

"Yo," Star says. "You got next."

"Maybe next time," Abby says, leading Dylan out of the kitchen by the hand.

Once again, Abby has Dylan in the passenger seat of her car.

She speeds away from the coast and is on the interstate before either of them speaks.

"Where are we going?"

Abby looks at the dashboard, checks her speed. "Taking a little ride."

"You didn't have to leave your own party."

Being alone with her is all Abby really wants anyway. Despite the obvious temptations of Star and Raven back there, being alone with Dylan will make it so much easier to determine if she's ready for the next step. "Most of those people will be there for two days. I'll catch up. Don't worry."

"I don't know what happened back there."

Abby looks at her over the top of her sunglasses.

"I mean, I can't explain it."

Contrition is a good sign and one Abby decides to exploit. "Well, ordinarily I'd say it's no big deal, but..."

"But what?"

Abby bites her lower lip and checks the pose in the rearview mirror. "Forget it," she says. "It's cheesy." She looks at Dylan, hoping to see inquisitiveness on her face. At first glance, she's stone-faced, as if she might drop the matter. Abby looks to the road and then back at her twice more.

Dylan finally says, "No, tell me."

Abby calculates the gamble and goes with the odds. Dylan's a woman after all. "Look, I know it's only been a week, but I want to be exclusive with you. You know? Is that crazy?"

"No," Dylan says, nearly coming out of her seat. "I don't know what to say, but I can say that it isn't crazy."

"So *we're* an *us,* right?"

"Appears so."

Abby loves this new development too much to reply.

After driving for what seems like a hundred miles with the liquor coursing in her veins and the sun blaring into the side mirror,

Dylan sees the muscles in Abby's forearms contract as she turns the wheel off the main road and onto a dry, unpaved trail. It's halfway through April and there has been little rain all spring. Chunky bits of shale crunch beneath the weight of the car as Abby rolls further into the wild, until she comes to a wide gate beneath a wrought iron arch with "Devonwood" spelled out in thick, black letters.

Abby parks as close to the metal fence as she can. Barbed wire runs endlessly in both directions.

"What is this?"

"It's a surprise," Abby says, getting out of the car.

After all she's been through, Dylan isn't much in the mood for surprises. She gets out of the car and walks to meet Abby at the gate, where Abby has a single key on a long piece of yarn that she's working into a weathered brass padlock thick as her fist.

Dylan hears crickets in the distance, their pulsing presence at about a four-hundred-megahertz hum. She recalls the cicadas when she'd lived in Virginia; they sounded like that, but not until July. The chirping, along with the sound of palm fronds brushing into each other in the wind, sounds like applause. This is interrupted by Abby clanging the lock, which she releases with a great click. "Swing that open for me, will you?"

Dylan complies, though she doesn't know exactly why, and walks through the heavy gate to the far side of a pathway leading into the palmetto bushes and pine trees.

The smell of strawberries growing in the fields to the east almost covers up the smell of the manure used to fertilize them. The alternating smells remind Dylan of childhood years when her father regularly ate Jell-O while farting in front of the television on the evenings he spent in port. At no other time have these two smells combined, and she can't help laughing now at the thought of it.

"What's so funny?"

"I think I'm drunk."

"Okay," Abby says, "it's just a short ride on the other side."

It's impossible for Dylan to distinguish whether the charge that runs through her is hesitation or excitement. She doesn't know Abby, really, has no idea what she might have planned back there. But for the first time in her life, she is part of a WE, and there is nowhere else to be. Above and beyond that tiny detail, she would walk through just about any kind of swamp to remain in Abby's company. And so, she does.

"What is this place?"

"Family property," Abby says. "My father calls this virgin land."

"Never been defiled by humans?"

"When my father inherited this property, it was nothing more than low-lying swampland. His bachelor uncle left it solely to him because he would know what to do with it." Her father used that rationality to section off the land in equal parts tradition and modernity. "There is a pretty big tree farm on the other side of 301, he keeps all kinds of animals in the corner by the Henderson property, and the rest is split pretty evenly between untouched land and tons of vegetables and garnishes for the Ru Maison."

"Giddyap," Dylan says.

"He charges rent, gets a cut of profits and all sorts of tax breaks, all while the value of the land increases."

"I understand how it works."

"He'll put all those people out of work one day. I know it. He'll negotiate some deal for a mall or jetport."

The gravel road ends before a drop in terrain. Beyond, Dylan can see the tops of reeds bowing in the faint breeze. "This is waterfront property?"

"We're too far east for the Hillsborough River. That's just a huge pond. It's spring-fed, but doesn't go anywhere."

"There alligators in there?"

"This is Florida. Of course there are. Last time I was here, I saw an eight-footer and three of her babies, but I don't know if they're still here. But relax. They don't fuck with you if you don't fuck with them first. Besides, we're going to the shed."

"Shed?"

"You'll see."

They get back in Abby's car and she shifts into drive while checking her lipstick in the rearview mirror.

Dylan braces herself in her seat as Abby flies down a gravel road.

"The smells from the strawberry farms make me think of my father," Dylan says.

"Is it the shit smell or the strawberry?"

"Both, actually."

"It's a couple thousand acres."

"That's a lot of strawberries."

"And a lot of shit they use for fertilizer. Some of it's organic, but most is still pumped in from tanks. It's cheaper nowadays to ship in chemicals. The real stuff was cheap and easy to get in the old days. There used to be a bunch of beef cattle out this way. Now though, development has chased the beef farmers away. They all ran off with big checks. There's only a couple of companies that grow strawberries locally anymore. They bought up everybody. And though those companies are family owned, they're big and rich. They've both tried to buy this land."

"I take it you're a conservationist."

"Me? I don't give a shit. Let them do what they want with it."

"The land or the fertilizer?"

"It's not my problem. Pave the land, genetically modify the food supply...whatever."

"That's pretty cynical."

"It's pragmatic. And fuck it. Seriously. It's not my battle to fight."

"What about the future?"

"Sweetheart, you are my future," Abby says, stopping the car between a house and the same pond they followed in.

"This is the hunting shed," she says walking toward the shed's door.

"You call this a shed?"

"Yeah, we do."

"How big is it?"

"About three thousand square feet. My father uses it to entertain his bigger clients and their guests for flora and fauna excursions."

"I meant how much land."

"It's just a little bigger than Central Park, but not the same shape."

"New York's Central Park?"

"But private."

"Wow."

"Don't be so awestruck. It's not a protected sanctuary or anything. It's more like his nest egg."

Three steps lead up to the solid oak front door—no decoration or molding, only another brass padlock attached to a steel hasp. Abby uses the same key she used on the gate and leads them into a room that opens to what otherwise might be a house if it had defined walls inside. There's a living room with couches and chairs set around a stacked-stone fireplace to the right and a kitchen in the back corner. A mahogany picnic table separates those two rooms from an assembly of bunk beds corralled on the opposite corner, adjacent to what appears to be a garage. Dylan sees tools and vehicles because the space lacks drywall. Seeing the wires running through the two-by-four studs makes her conscious for the first time that there are lights on in the place, even as sunlight streams through the many windows.

"I know for a fact that no one has been here for over a month. Do you know how much electricity they've wasted leaving all these lights on?"

"That's got to be expensive for somebody."

"They don't care. My father has people who write out his bills. He can't be bothered to mind details like this."

Dylan follows Abby toward the kitchen, where she opens the

refrigerator. "What is this place?" she asks.

"I told you, it's the hunting shed."

What Abby calls a "shed" is more accurately some sort of a lodge. The ceiling is constructed with exposed wood beams and a number of commercial lighting fixtures, mostly fluorescent, with three window-mounted air conditioners, all blowing cold air. She takes a seat on a couch by the fireplace.

"It's hardly a shed." Dylan looks at the bare walls and the terrazzo flooring. In the center of the expansive structure, two beams support the ceiling on either side of the front door.

Abby hasn't been there in weeks, but the place is still clean and nice and cool. She walks in as if nothing is wrong, but she's still concerned about this little distraction.

"This hunting shed means more to my father than life itself. It's the only refuge he has, and he's been known to disappear here for a week at a time. I was never allowed to come here as a girl. I'm not supposed to be here now, but that's just tough shit for everyone. I use the place as a getaway from Lawton some-times. Like now. Plus, I get to bring you here so we can both be ourselves."

The last time Abby found herself there was a couple of months earlier, when she'd called an electrician. She'd smoked a joint on the steps leading to the hunting shed while she waited for him to pull up the drive in his white van with TECO emblazoned across the side. The guy kept his face well groomed. He stood a little short and stocky, but thick enough in the right areas to make up for it.

She wasted no time offering a hit of the joint, and though he initially reached for it, he ultimately declined. Abby'd stubbed it out on the railing and showed him to the breaker box in the garage.

He had light hair and "Tampa Electric Co." embroidered in red above the pocket on one side of his tan shirt, and "Dan" stitched above the other. "What seems to be the problem?" he asked.

She leaned on the hot water heater, looked at the snuffed out joint and said, "If there's a surge or something out here, it could be deadly, right?"

"The breaker would trip before any real damage could be done."

Abby batted her eyelashes at him. "Is there a way around that?"

The guy paused, looked at her. "No. It's pretty failsafe."

"I mean, *could* there be a way around that?"

"I don't understand."

Abby reached out and untucked the long tails of his company shirt. She'd dealt with this kind of guy at Rifley's thousands of times. He impressed her as the type who would act all cool until halfway through a lap dance, when he'd pop in his pants.

She pulled him toward her, sucked hickey-tight on his neck, stripped off his shirt, stroked his crotch. "Just rig it so it won't trip."

"I don't know."

Abby sank to her knees, pulled down his pants and undershorts, and took him in her mouth. Dan squeezed her head and ground into her face, and she knew he'd do whatever she asked.

The electrician's jizz repulsed her. Instead of swallowing him, she snowballed the wad back into his mouth with a deep kiss. He tried to flinch away, but she had him gripped in her arms. "That's so hot, baby," she said. "So hot." She'd dated a guy in construction a couple summers ago and knew he'd buy it. She didn't know if he did so to impress her or turn her on, but afterward, she wiped her mouth on his shirt and then tossed it into his general direction, not caring if he caught it or not.

Afterward, she watched him replace the fuse with a steel rod the size of her finger and rig the breaker with a garbage bag twist tie. She could tell he wanted to ask what she had planned, but they left the deal simple. She wouldn't tell anyone he'd been there, and he'd deny ever being there.

Her kind words and warm mouth were like magical powers. She knew it wasn't fair, but as long as she got what she wanted, it made no difference.

Abby says, "Come with me," and leads Dylan into the only sectioned off area in the hunting shed, which is a large room with three rows of bunk beds and a queen-size bed beneath the window. Within that room, another little room makes up the only bathroom.

She slides onto the bed as Dylan stands over her. She grazes Dylan's arm with a finger. She's seen Dylan's scars. Her blood. As enigmatic as Dylan is, she knows her, if not better than anyone else, then at least better than she currently knows anyone else.

"You know what?" Abby says. "We don't have drinks. There's the better part of a full bar in the cabinet by the sink in the island."

"I don't drink. You," Dylan stops, looks at her, "can drink anything you want, of course." Dylan stands like a schoolgirl called upon for an answer. "I didn't mean to imply that you...I mean...I just don't drink. That's all."

Abby wonders if she feels as awkward as she looks, standing there. "You were slamming them pretty good out of Raven's belly button a while ago."

"Like I said, I can't explain it. Though I feel it now."

"What about at the bar last week?"

"Water." Dylan sits down and rubs her palms on her khaki-covered thighs.

"What about the wine at lunch the other day?"

"I left my glass for the cleaning lady. You finished the bottle."

Great, Abby thinks. Another wagon-rider who will shit all over the place when she trips on one of the twelve steps. Abby's been with two of those types and seriously hopes Dylan won't be number three. She stands and turns her back to Dylan as she moves to her purse on the tall chest of drawers on the far side of the room. "Is that some sort of choice or have you had a problem in the past?"

"My father," Dylan stammers.

Keeping her back to Dylan, Abby reaches into her purse for the baggie of weed Awesome Sanchez sold her on his way into the party. "Go on."

"My father was an alcoholic."

It's then that the tone of her voice registers embarrassment. Fear. Abby turns. "And you're afraid of having the gene."

Dylan makes eye contact, that fiercely honest eye contact. "Something like that."

"My parents are chronic medicators. Always have been," Abby says, opening the baggie and breathing in the smell of weed. "Booze is a killer."

"What are you doing?" Dylan sounds panicked as she stands, peeking in.

Not looking up from her task, Abby says, "Rolling a joint. What's it look like?" She bites on one of her fake nails. "If it weren't for these damn things, I'd be done by now." Bent over the table, she cranks her neck to look at Dylan. "Oh, you're bringing up the irony." She gestures to the bag of weed on the desk before turning her attention back to the task. "Having just talked about my parents self-medicating and now I've got this. I know. It's funny." She flips her hair over her shoulder and finishes rolling the joint. "But that's different. They're into pills, you know? Instead of accepting reality, they mask it with pills. They medicate the 'now' with the 'what ought to be.' It's total bullshit. Like living on a Hollywood set." She picks weed off the stem like a buzzard getting meat from roadkill. She rolls and talks. "High cholesterol?" she says, gesturing toward her heart. "Pill." She grabs her crotch. "Can't get it up? Take a pill." Her hands go back to her hips. "Weight gain? Pill. Holding onto a little water? Pill. Stress? Hangover? Hyperactivity? Pill. Pill. Pill. Total fucking manipulation of reality. Instead of facing pain or any other problems, they medicate." She picks up the joint and hands it to Dylan. "You have a light?"

"I don't know," Dylan says, one hand giving that *stop* signal.

"Don't tell me you don't get high, either." Abby ends the statement with a smile.

"I don't know what to say here."

Abby crosses the bunk room and leads Dylan to the big bed, where she folds one leg under her and sits facing Dylan. "You just get more precious with each passing minute. You know that?" She throws her arms around Dylan's neck and hugs her. Hormones surge when she hugs back. With her arms squeezing her, Dylan leans her head over Abby's shoulder until she breaks the grip. "After you smoke a bit of this," Abby says, "you'll just say whatever comes to your mind."

Dylan doesn't say no.

Dylan's coughing fit is intense, and the more she coughs, the higher she gets. "You're lifted," Abby says. "And I have to warn you about the inevitable laughing fit."

Dylan hears her own breathing, audible over the whisper of the wall unit air conditioner blowing cold air over them. She looks at the tiny sliver of light beaming through the gap in the blackout blinds. Beneath the window, an old pub table stands with one wooden chair pushed in toward the wall. The height and color of the chair remind her of a similar one she had in her room growing up. Not just a chair, it became a refuge where she'd sit and rock herself during the recovery phase of her punishments. She didn't know until she grew older that those periods of time when her father stopped hitting her and ordered her to her room stemmed either from the old man's fear of pounding her to death or that she'd begin liking the pain. Dylan grew to love the embrace of that chair, because nothing else ever made her feel good in those early years.

Huddled on the bed, Abby says, "Tell me something about

you that I couldn't possibly know."

Dylan can't. No matter how easy it would be to open up in that moment, in that room, in the presence of that little chair. Instead, she offers, "This is the first relationship I've had."

Abby traces a scar along the right side of Dylan's torso. "I think this scar is an hourglass. I believe it symbolizes the fact we're going to spend a lot of time together."

"I wouldn't mind you being correct."

As Dylan leans against the pillows on the bed, she says, "Bribes of peach milkshakes from Baldwin's Creamery in Mill Cove will do you no good."

"What?" Abby laughs.

"I'm not inclined to discuss the unrest in my mind. And I don't have to discuss the spinning or the weightlessness beneath my feet that pushes me upward in a chilled raft. But you know what? Now speaking is no longer pleasant." Dylan lets out a string of giggles, and the more she laughs the more it *makes* her laugh until she rolls off the bed onto the floor. The sound of her laughter makes Abby laugh.

Abby contents herself by lying next to Dylan on the floor. Dylan's high, and in between the laughing fits, Abby wonders if she has a serious candidate on her hands and not just another pretender.

Abby tries to control her hands. Dylan should make the first move, but she just lies there, arms at her side, as if cold. Abby's resolve isn't as strong as it might be if not for the weed and the beers she had earlier. There's an impulse to catch Dylan before she starts laughing again. Abby rolls on top of her and feels Dylan's belt buckle against the taut span of her jean shorts. She slides down a few inches and gyrates in no uncertain terms. She's ready. It's been almost a week and she needs it. Dylan is the oldest woman she's been with since last summer, but after a week, she has to be ready, too.

Abby slides her hand up and down the length of a khaki-covered leg, leans up and kisses Dylan. The residual smile, leftover from her laughing, turns into a pucker and then a sloppy, open-mouth kiss. She pushes herself away and Dylan lies there, motionless, so Abby takes complete control, pins Dylan's arms to the floor beside her head, and restrains herself from attempting another kiss. The moment Abby relaxes her grip on Dylan's arms, Dylan clamps them along her sides again. If she doesn't realize she's got nothing to be embarrassed of by this point in her life, she never will. And the deeper Abby looks, somehow Dylan's different now. Softer. There's less energy in her face. Less rage in her eyes. In place of the dominance that had blazed there that first night, sadness hangs about her now. Not just sadness, but fear.

Abby can use this.

Abby buries her nose in Dylan's hair. "It's okay." She licks Dylan's face and grinds her pubic mound into her belt buckle, feels her cervix thumping fluid to the surface, getting wetter by the second.

Dylan enters another giggling fit. With her arms pinned to her side and Abby straddling her, all that moves is her abdomen and ribs. They swell and tighten with laughter as Abby slides off her, but she doesn't stop. Instead of waiting, Abby unbuckles Dylan's belt, tugs down her zipper, pulls down her pants.

Dylan's done with the giggling at this point, but Abby wishes she'd held her to just two hits of the joint. Her eyes are too squinty to have that fire in them like they did last time, but Abby aches too much to care. It's not Dylan's eyes that matter, so Abby ignores the laugh track as she lowers her mouth to Dylan's mound. Abby wiggles herself out of her shorts. With one hand around Dylan's waist, she uses the other to wipe a handful of wetness with the tail of her shirt before scooting around to scissor her, feeling the carpet beneath an outstretched knee.

Dylan's laughter increases in both momentum and volume as Abby positions herself forward, once, twice, and then settles back. She's practically howling as Abby reaches and then stuffs her shorts in Dylan's mouth as she grinds into her, feet flat on the floor, knees in her chin, grasping Dylan's shirt collar like a bridle. Her sore ankle is not even a thought. Last time she never got on top, but now she can take her time and tease her. Endurance like hers could prove challenging, but given enough time, she might just be able to prove her a mere mortal. Then, Abby comes. It is deep and rich and satisfyingly wet, and Abby's amazed it got so intense so fast. "You don't have to last as long as last time," she says. "We'll both be very sore if you do."

Dylan spits out the shorts Abby stuffed in her mouth and her laughter finds volume, which snuffs Abby out like a cold wind. Abby slides off. She sits on the floor beside Dylan and hugs her knees to her chest. "I knew I should have held you to two hits."

The nylon fibers of the carpet have indented her hands and knees and she rubs them with her fingertips until Dylan understands.

She pushes herself up from the floor and disappears into the bathroom.

Before Dylan can rise and dress, Abby exits the bathroom holding a disposable razor wrapped in cellophane. She waves the blue plastic handle in her hand. "I'll be right back," she says, walking naked through the bunk room and into the open space of the garage.

Dylan wonders if she's planning to groom herself right there and then, but there isn't any hair on Abby's body. Dylan wonders if she expects to groom her. Instead, Abby reenters the bunk room still holding the blue plastic razor, but in her other hand, she has a pair of red-handled pliers.

Dylan makes her way up and sits back on the bed and watches with raging curiosity as Abby nips and pries at the razor. After a modest struggle, she proclaims, "Voila!" as she extracts a length of shiny metal blade. She looks up at Dylan, a sensual smile spread across her angled lips. "I've got something special for you. Lie back."

Abby kneels down between Dylan's legs and hovers her mouth inches from Dylan's crotch. What has Dylan's attention is the razor blade in Abby's hand, held in such close proximity to the outside of her thigh. Abby simultaneously lowers both her mouth and the razor, and the mix of sensations sends current like lightning bolts into Dylan's clenched toes. It is otherworldly; she can't believe the intensity.

With one hand holding the blade, the other fondles Dylan's folds as Abby plays her mouth up and down, licking, biting, sucking, and ultimately cutting into Dylan's leg, just below the space her right pocket would be. The pain and pleasure are intense, and at once she's more aroused than she's ever been. Dylan locks in a stare with Abby—bonding in that moment. If magnetism drew them together, this serves as the arch that welds them together. It's as if Abby knew what Dylan really wanted even though she didn't know it herself. Sharing this with her is magical, but it's over so quickly. Blood and wetness being brought to bear at Abby's hands instead of her own makes Dylan fall completely and irrevocably in love with her. She is not only the first woman interested in sharing that part with her, but she seemed to take pleasure in doing so.

An hour later, they ride matching ATVs from the shed. Both machines are covered in camouflage. They motor around the pond near the road and into the heart of the property. Dylan is not the least apprehensive, because she'd do anything to prove herself worthy of the woman beside her.

There is a main path as they ride, but sometimes Abby deviates through palmetto bushes, over cypress knees and a small stream, as if she has a specific destination in mind. Dylan's no longer holding a semblance of the weed buzz, but the jolts over the rough terrain bump her newest wound and slosh the booze still in her stomach.

Through hundreds of acres of woodland, area as dense as jungles, Abby finally brings her ATV to a stop near the corner of a fence that borders another pond with a rolling stream. She withdraws from a holster on her ATV what at first appears to be a rifle. A charge of familiarity surges through Dylan's hands as she's handed a crossbow. It reminds her of the M4 Carbine that got her through Iraq. She hasn't thought about her battle weapon in years, yet here she is holding another, though decidedly different, weapon.

Instead of a full-auto switch, a complicated pulley system attaches where the barrel would be. The stock is painted jungle camouflage and there is a four-arrow quiver built into its side. There's one loaded in the chamber. It's not the 5.56 mm she'd gotten used to, but she's curious. "What am I supposed to do with this?"

"Shhh." Abby's lips twist, then in a low voice she says, "Let's duck through that clearing."

Dylan keeps up well, sucking through the mud in her loafers. She'd rather have her Boondockers, but she's intrigued as she follows Abby though a clearing overlooking the pond. Abby points. Drinking from the opposite shore is a deer.

"Take your shot," Abby whispers.

Though Dylan's seen crossbows on television and in movies, she's never actually held one before, and she's surprised by how small it is. "Cock it here," Abby says, "and it's ready to go."

The feel of the rifle stock pressed into Dylan's shoulder is as familiar a feeling as a baseball bat in a retired player's hands. She's suddenly captivated by the tip of the arrow, which holds a pyramid of three serrated blades that gleam in falling sunlight. She studies them and rubs the new wound Abby cut and bandaged a little while ago.

As branches of oaks and pines wave overhead, she drops to one knee for a better firing base, re-shoulders the crossbow, and zeros in with precision and comfort. Experience coming back to her. She qualified accurate up to five hundred yards with her M4, but has no idea what this crossbow thing can do. The deer is no more than fifty yards ahead through the brush, down among the mangroves drinking from the pond.

"Take the shot," Abby says in a whisper through closed teeth.

Dylan lines up the shot through the graduated Nikon scope. She's used to dual-aperture sights, so the Nikon scope makes her job even easier. She squeezes the trigger and realizes she forgot to cock the damn thing. A boot camp mistake, but for all her training and experience, this particular technology is new to her.

Abby moans, but they are relived that the deer has failed to notice.

Dylan cocks the bow, settles down onto her elbows, and sights the animal again. She has no overwhelming urge to take the shot, but Abby's next to her, like a spotter who's got Dylan's six, and the last thing on her mind is disappointing Abby.

With the deer in the sights, Dylan holds her breath and squeezes the trigger. The deer springs up and flees a hundred feet, and then drops to the wet earth just outside the shade.

"You must have hit an organ."

"Spinal cord," Dylan says as matter of fact as the time of day, but she wouldn't be able to explain what she's feeling even if she were inclined to share it with Abby. She doesn't understand it herself. It has been so long since she's felt the sensation of living by taking a life. She is stronger for having taken the shot. This is a gift she'll forever be grateful for.

"You're good at this," Abby says.

"Is it usually difficult?" Dylan asks while looking over the crossbow, wondering if she can break it down and clean it as if it were an M4. She owes this feeling to Abby, and though she won't tell her that she feels more alive than she has in years, she will enjoy it when Abby isn't looking.

Abby pauses and thinks better of telling Dylan how anyone's

first kill is at least somewhat emotional—pity or pride, there is usually something. Abby first killed a bird in the backyard. She had grabbed Lawton's water rifle as she walked outside with her mother to get the mail. She happened upon a bird nestled in the thick grass and shot it like Daniel Boone because that's what she thought she was supposed to do with wildlife. The water didn't seem to do the job, so Abby turned the gun around and began chopping at the bird with the wider end. Her mother ran over to stop her, but it came too late. With mail fluttering to the ground, Abby got her first look at death. She cried for days after that. But now, Dylan isn't letting on that shooting a deer even registers. "Well, that will mess up somebody's bookkeeping," Abby says.

"You mean you rank them?"

"That was a Key deer. Only three hundred left in the state. My father had five brought out here."

"You said this wasn't a sanctuary," Dylan says. Her voice comes out low and lacks any kind of emotion.

"The herd surely won't miss him. They're not that smart. No one will know it was you." As they walk toward the deer, Abby says, "These aren't God's creatures. They're baubles, novelties. Items. Nothing more."

Dylan tugs out the arrow from the spinal cord, just behind the skull. She wipes blood and sinew on the pine needles at their feet in an effort to remove the evidence.

"Doing this," Abby says, "proves you're even more perfect for me than I thought."

"Really?" Dylan says. She puts the arrow in place as she reloads the crossbow and squats down.

"What are you doing?" Abby asks, something like panic in her voice.

"Shhh," Dylan says. "I'm more perfect for you than you ever imagined."

Six

Cleve Bejeak hears the call come in over the police scanner he keeps on his dead wife's pie table next to his recliner: "Three deer, each with single point of entry wounds found on the Stratton Plain called Devonwood." The old lady would shit if she knew her prized antique served as a podium for such violence and mayhem, but she's dead and the police scanner is all that Cleve has beside scotch and biographies of dead presidents. The call coming across makes him close his book and put down his drink.

As he arrives on the scene twenty minutes later, there are two county cop cars near the gate on Faulkenburg Road, along with three Fish and Game SUVs.

Cleve's orthopedic shoes sink into the dank mud on the outskirts of the vast refuge of old-time Florida wilderness owned by the richest son of a bitch in Hillsborough County.

"Cleve? Is that you?" a heavyset deputy named Thompson says from amongst a huddle of the clueless in uniform. He's got a baby face, but one cheek bulges from a wad of chewing tobacco. "What are you doing here?"

Cleve approaches the group standing by the wire fence. "I was in the area and thought I'd stop by."

Thompson spits into the rough near the gatepost. "That's no way to live your retirement. But it's good to see you," he says. "Do you all know Detective Bejeak?"

Cleve interrupts any semblance of recognition by saying, "Former detective. I'm retired." Cleve retired a detective, but he'd gotten promoted to that rank only two years prior—the oldest deputy to be appointed detective in department history. Everyone considered his work solid, but admittedly slow. Not mentally challenged, but rather meticulous. Everything he did took longer than anyone else in the department. He only had a fraction of the arrests his fellow deputies had, but his conviction rate was one hundred percent. His record of one hundred percent accuracy served as his saving grace all his years in the department. On balance, this proved for a respectable career.

After those assembled nod acknowledgement and take turns shaking Cleve's hand, he repeats what he heard on the scanner. "Single entry wound took down each of these animals?"

"There's blood, but no lead best we can tell."

"You think it might be kids?"

"Kids with jackknives or something?" a skinny, female "fish and gamer" asks. "I don't know."

Cleve plods through the moist earth to the carcass of one of the dead deer lying prone along the fence. A swarm of flies buzz about his head as he nears. Birds have long since gotten the dead animal's eyes, leaving moist holes and fragments of connective tissue. Cleve bends, then squats. The wound is obvious, with a trail of blood staining the blond fur. "Who would kill such a beautiful animal?" Cleve says, rubbing the animal between its empty eye sockets. The dead deer's face looks almost comforted.

"This far out in the country, all sorts of strange shit happens," Thompson says.

"This isn't a stab wound," Cleve says, pulling back the deer's fur. "Too much force. I've seen plenty of stabbings in my days. This ain't a stabbing. Besides, who could get close enough?"

"Deers are skittish," Thompson says. The fish and gamers all grumble and add their two cents on the issue.

"Whoever did this is long gone, too. I can tell you that. They didn't want venison or they would have taken the fucking things."

"Such a damn shame," the female fish and gamer says.

"What about a knife thrower?" Thompson says, spitting a

stream of Red Man onto the ground. "You reckon someone could be that accurate?"

"Yeah, a ninja came all the way out here to sniff nature and snuff deer," the female fish and gamer says.

"Don't get nasty," Thompson says.

"A single, fatal entry wound on each of them—Money Bags Stratton been out here lately?" Cleve asks.

"He made a statement over the phone that he ain't been here since February."

Cleve thinks it's a crime to own this land and not spend time on it. "Who reported this?"

"Caretakers," the female fish and gamer says.

"Did Stratton have any guests out here?"

"Come on, Cleve. Go on back home. This is no way to spend your retirement. Go play golf. Let us worry about all this," Thompson says, and spits.

On Monday afternoon, Lawton unhitches the trailer from his pickup and drives to Tampa to meet his buddy Elliot at Mom's diner on Dale Mabry Highway.

He arrives early and sits in a booth within eyeshot of the counter where a girl leans on a stool, showing off the backs of her legs. He wishes she had been at his party, but for now he's content staring at her while pretending to read a menu.

The girl turns around after a few minutes and locks eyes with Lawton, who waves at her, suggesting she join him.

A waitress comes by with a coffee pot and cup. "That's my daughter, and she's only seventeen."

"That's cool. I was just saying hello."

"Right," she says, filling his coffee cup.

A moment later, a bell clangs as Elliot enters. He wears his Air Force dress uniform and removes his hat the second one shined shoe touches the linoleum in the diner.

"Thanks for meeting me," Lawton says.

"You look like shit."

"Alcohol flu. Probably shouldn't even be driving."

"Your party was that good, huh?"

"Epic. You missed an all-out blow-out."

"Rub it in," Elliot says, waving the waitress over by signaling for coffee.

"I hate to cut you short, but I'm suffering here. What did you find for me?" Lawton uses his friend to check out certain clients who piss him off, as well as the people his sister sees while she's in town. He doesn't like what she's up to. Though he doesn't know for sure, he can't risk Abby hanging around the wrong kind of guys or girls. Having a friend like Elliot makes it as easy as looking in her wallet: driver's license number, credit cards, and paper business cards. Down at MacDill Air Force Base, Elliot pulls reports from banks, credit companies, and military dependent status.

"Dude," Elliot, says. "This chick's all-American. She was a Navy chief's dependent as a kid and a Marine for a couple years. College degree on the G.I. Bill, held the same job for over a decade. No arrests, not even a speeding ticket. She's begged off jury duty twice, but she's got strong credit. And, get this, she's single, but she owns a house and is sitting on a six-figure savings account. It's a portfolio, really, like a potato baked twice and stuffed once; you know what I mean?"

"Really?" Lawton sits back, the vinyl booth sticking to his skin. "You ought to see this woman. She's a freak. All scarred up."

The waitress pours coffee, pretending not to hear any of their conversation.

"You mean like burned and shit?"

"No, I mean like scarification." He slurps coffee. "You know, rituals or something."

"That's fucked up."

"You know?" Lawton slurps again.

"What are you going to do?"

"I'll just make sure she doesn't hang around too much or too long, you know?"

"It's probably a good idea."

"I mean, I can't babysit Abby when she's out of the country, but I can damn sure keep an eye on her when she's in town."

"I'm telling you, put in a good word for me and she'll be well supervised."

"Don't fuck with me," Lawton says. "I think I've done major brain damage."

"I wish I could've made it to your party."

"You should have sold your shift."

"SinTel came down special to survey the information we put together last week."

"Sounds fun. I've got to go, but thanks for looking at this chick."

"What about breakfast?"

"Are you insane? I can't eat."

"You're supposed to buy."

Lawton takes out a crumpled twenty-dollar bill and tosses it on the table. "All right, man. I'll talk to you later. And thanks again for the info."

"Keep an eye on Abby," Elliot says as the bell jangles on Lawton's way out.

To learn the whereabouts of the Stratton family during the typical day, Cleve Bejeak has his buddy at the sheriff's office run a cross-check. Mr. Stratton has eleven corporations attached to his name, and after some digging, Cleve learns the building he spends the most time in is also the tallest in downtown Tampa. Mrs. Stratton doesn't work. Instead, she can alternately be found at the yacht club, golf club, one of various charity events or, more often than not, at the private shopping areas of Saks Fifth Avenue or Nordstrom. Her son runs a lawn care service under an LLC, but the daughter has no recent W-2 history. There is information indicating an eight-figure trust in each of their names. And though they're entitled to draw from them as they see fit, they remain untapped, with all interest and dividends fed back into them, making them grow even larger.

Cleve has an address, so he stakes out the house that brother and sister own together in Pinellas Park. Eight hours he sits there, his car parked under the shade of a banyan tree that harbors birds with active bowels. Droppings land like wet gunfire on the hood, trunk, and roof before the Stratton girl finally exits the house.

Following her means he never sees her face, but for now he can dial into her dark hair visible in the rear window of her car. He follows at a distance, not close enough to be noticed.

On the way into Rifley's, traffic across the bridge is heavy for a Wednesday night, and by the time Abby gets to the three steps in back of the building, she's late for Zoe's shift.

Abby doesn't want to be there. She doesn't care about Zoe or her aunt or whatever, but she couldn't pull a no-show and fuck the girl over. Besides, it's the one-time Rifley actually got to write her name onto the schedule board himself. She can't let him down either. She isn't bitter about that; she just wants to be with Dylan. Never before has she gotten so close so quickly to a man or a woman, and she fears Dylan might get away just as quickly. Abby feels good about having Dylan wrapped up for the moment based on recent events they shared, but anybody who's into the kind of radical shit she is can be considered unpredictable, at best.

"Four hours," Abby tells herself, facing Rifley's cold gray stage door. "If I'm not making killer money, in four hours I'll leave."

Standing there she hears car horns and tires on the pavement in a steady rush of traffic heading south into the city. She notices the peeling, gray paint on the thick metal door. She's never taken the time to see it before, but today it looks like petals opening from a flannel rose. It's a laughable image in her brain, and it's then she realizes how much she will miss this place.

Inside, the velvet-covered benches along the back wall are enveloped in the red haze of the house lights. It's already seven thirty, and in the dressing room the girls are still talking about Abby's party. When she walks in, they all stop and applaud her.

Star stops brushing glitter onto to her eyelids and neck, gets up from her stool in front of the mirror, and hugs Abby. "Girl, that party set some kind of record."

The other girls chime in with, "Yeahs" and "Uh-huhs."

"It was more fun for me," Abby says, tempted to tell them what she did with Dylan out in Plant City while they were getting drunk and grab-assing. "I'm glad you all had a good time, even you, Star."

"I didn't even know about the party," Bunny says from her seat on the couch.

Unlike most of the other girls, Bunny is conscripted to Rifley. She has an all-inclusive deal with room and board at a one-bedroom place not far away. This way she never goes homeless or hungry no matter how far she snorts herself into the hole.

Abby hates Bunny because she's danced for so long that she's the only one who takes herself seriously. She is the ghost of stripper future and Abby doesn't like what she sees: still good-looking, still in great shape, still dancing...what then? Does she retire when she feels the time is right? Will she notice a steady decline in her earnings? Being conscripted to Rifley, it would hardly matter unless customers ridiculed her every night.

"What's that supposed to mean, *even me?*" Star asks.

"I'm just a little on edge is all. Besides, you tried to get my date fucked up and I needed her sober."

"She's all right," Star says, taking her seat. "But she ain't worth getting so fucked up over so quickly if you ask me."

"I didn't ask you," Abby says, slamming down a hairbrush on the makeup counter. "And I don't need your shit. I'm only here tonight, Star, because of you. I'm doing this for you, remember? So don't fuck with me."

"Yo. Lighten up. Shit, girl. It's cool."

Abby fights the surge to her head and heart and breathes in and out. She isn't mad at Star so much as she's shaken by what might have happened if she'd gotten to Dylan too late.

Chardonnay, being the youngest and least comfortable with confrontation, speaks up in an obvious attempt to change the subject. "I want to be somebody else today."

"Step into my salon," Abby says, exhaling aggression and dusting off the stool nearest her. "I'll give you a mini-makeover."

And as Bunny sulks away to the bathroom, Abby cuts Chardonnay's bangs, long and feathery. "How do you feel about retro?"

"Hey, Cassandra," Chardonnay says. "Would you please work for me on the twenty-ninth?"

"I don't think so."

"Just this once? I've got a rich kid's prom to go to."

"Find somebody else to ask. I might be going somewhere." It's as much an explanation as Abby wants to give.

Cleve Bejeak waited until half past ten to enter Rifley's Eden. It was the first time he'd been in there, but it wasn't so different from other strip clubs he'd seen back in his day. He finds a seat near the door and watches the girls take the stage. He laughs when a cocktail waitress with fishnet stockings and a little coat with tails tells him, "Totally nude means no liquor, just juice and soda. Because of the old blue laws that's all we're allowed to serve."

The strongest drink they serve there is club soda, so he sips from the glass now and again while looking at all the women. Instead of ogling their naked bodies, he occupies himself by trying to match the dancers' faces to the photo of Abigail Stratton that he found on file at the *Tribune*. The photo is a number of years old, and though crystal clear, the makeup, hair, and lighting make Cleve have to study each face. The nudity stirs something in him, but all that comes of it is three trips to urinate.

For Abby, dancing is a strange balance of aggression and submission, but no matter her mood, it is always physical. Amid the spotlights and applause, she swings around the pole with a roundhouse kick.

Today is busier than most Wednesday evenings, packed with suits and uniforms gathered together to throw money at nude women just for being nude. The execs and trades will be turned on for their twenty-dollar cover charge, nourished by the ten-dollar buffet, with a lap dance or a trip to the VIP room for dessert.

In the third hour of Abby's shift, she's all smiles and relatively anonymous in her black wig, but she's wishing she'd gone with the Ace wrap beneath her boots. Her ankle is sore and swelling.

With the injury, coming back to the stage after even a thirty-minute break makes every twinge in her back remind her that the gelatin in her joints is eroding. It's only a matter of a few years before bone grinds arthritic bone and vertebrae, then collapses with osteoporosis. Nothing hurt in her younger days, nothing. A life lived healthy and pampered, and when not completely healthy, she got pampered even more. All discomfort pacified. Rectified.

But now, things are different.

In the beginning, Edison Winthrop went to Rifley's only when his wife traveled to her mother's with the kids. Through the decades, his patronage varied from once per month or as much as five days straight. Since Rifley's is a "juice joint" any of the patrons who are drunk like Winthrop came in that way.

From his usual seat behind the left corner of the stage, he

sips a cranberry juice and feels it mix with the vodka he keeps in his car under the driver's seat.

Of all his trips in to Rifley's, the girl he catches less frequently than all the others is the auburn-haired hottie called Cassandra. In addition to the beauty and the happy coincidence of seeing her there, she also has, along with overt sexuality, a seductive quality the other girls lack. Perhaps if she were there more often he'd notice her less and focus his attention on one of the big-titted blondes. There are plenty of those in the rotation, and Winthrop likes it that way. For a Wednesday, Rifley's has a stellar cast on duty.

It's eleven thirty and Winthrop has board meetings in the morning, but sleep is less valuable than this kind of stimulation.

Cassandra ends her set with a cowgirl finale to a ZZ Top song. She bucks the pole sensually and crawls and spreads, and on the last two notes, pyrotechnics of some sort pop from right and left of stage. The whole bar is lit like daytime, and in the bright light clarity he recognizes the face. He leans closer, making the association. He'd never believe it, except that he saw her only last week, in Dylan Rivers's cubicle of all places. She brought lunch.

Before Abby makes it to the dressing room, Winthrop grabs her arm. "I want a private dance."

She pretends she doesn't recognize Winthrop, his tie loosened around his neck and the top button of his oxford shirt undone. Her ankle hurts, but like a cleaning service or a masseuse, she is for hire, and it is the necessary evil of sexual fantasy. "I'll be right back." If she has to delay the attention to her ankle she'll live, but she really wants to ditch having to dance for him.

"Now," Winthrop says, waving a wad of bills in her face.

The suits at the table behind them cheer him on, grunting some two-syllable name like unintelligible apes.

She doesn't know which bouncer is working the door.

He's just here for the show, she tells herself, and smiles at him and winks. "All right, honey," she says. "Let's go." She's sure her Louise Brooks wig, white frosted eye shadow, high and wide on the lids, heavy black pencil and false lashes like tarantulas will be an adequate disguise.

Winthrop walks fast and stumbles into a table on the way. It's hard to tell if he's drunk or just anxious. He's moving quickly, but he hunches every time his foot or knee bumps into a chair on his way to the VIP room.

Once inside, Abby sets him on a leather bench along the back wall. Chardonnay is on the other side of the room with a trade guy, finishing off an orgasm of her own by humping his shoulder. She can do it on a guy's knee too, but she generally earns higher if she uses his shoulder or bald head.

As Chardonnay and her man leave the VIP room, Abby squats down in front of Winthrop and spreads his knees apart. Her ankle is tight as it stretches in this new position, but it's bearing her weight okay. She rubs her hands up his thighs as she rises to fly her nipples across his facial airspace. He reaches up, cups her breasts.

Shit like this is something she will not miss. Attention and cheers, fine. Grabbing and demanding, not fine.

She grabs his narrow shoulders in her hands and closes his knees with her own as she straddles him, and after double-checking that his zipper is closed, she grinds into him. Smearing herself, hoping she stains his pants. She doesn't recall seeing a ring on his finger, but she hopes he's got a disagreeable wife at home whom he'll have to explain this to. The thought makes her smile as she tosses her head, slinging wig hair away from her face to look at his.

"Hump my leg, Abigail," he says.

Abby flips her hair back into her face with two quick tugs and says, "I'm Cassandra, honey. Everybody knows me."

"Yeah. I know you. And after you clean your cunt on my leg, you're going to take out my prick and climb on it. Just like your pretty little mama does to your daddy."

Abby slaps Winthrop with an open palm. Before she can get in another swing, she's tossed to the couch by a punch of his own that connects right below her left eye.

She pushes herself up and lunges with her forearm and plants it in his throat. He gurgles once, then again as she reaches down and grabs whatever he's got down there. She squeezes his dick until he hyperventilates and reaches for his pills. Abby knocks them away and then kicks them with her foot. She applies more pressure and forces him to sit on the sofa, all the while twisting her grip. To his gurgling, Winthrop adds moaning loud enough to make Abby muffle his mouth with a pillow until he stops squirming.

After a number of sets, Cleve watches the woman he has pegged as Abigail walk into the VIP area with a man roughly as old as himself. A short while after that, he hears a woman's voice call out, barely perceptible, but distinct in its urgency. His ear traces the truncated sound to the VIP room.

"That son of a bitch," Cleve says, abandoning his table, leaving his half-full club soda. He trots to the door to the little room. Without the spotlights, it's dark inside and it takes a moment for Cleve's eyes to adjust. He sees a woman bent over a man who's reclining on a sofa.

"Abigail Stratton?" Cleve says. The wig threw him for the first two sets she danced, but he knows it's her from the newspaper photo. At this range, he realizes for the first time that he also recognizes her from his nephew's funeral ten days ago. He instantly begins to ponder. He wonders if there's a common thread between his nephew, Vincent, and the dead deer on the Stratton property. But he still has no idea why Stratton's daughter would be stripping when she has twelve million dollars at her disposal.

"He hit me," she says.

"I believe you." He wants to pick up that old son of a bitch and throttle him for laying as much as a finger on her. "Why don't you get out of here and let me handle this?"

"Who are you?"

"Don't concern yourself with that now. Just make yourself scarce." He watches the hemispheres of her ass undulate as she walks out of the room without saying another word. With the door closed behind her, he turns his attention to the man on the sofa.

Abby makes record time across the Sunshine Skyway Bridge and down I-75. Traffic is light and she's a bullet flying to her target. It's one a.m. by the time she gets to the exit at Temple Terrace, and she gears down and runs the red light shining bright in the dark night air. She doesn't believe in GPS and so navigates her way by the street signs until she finds the road she's looking for, Applebee Place, in a modest subdivision of single-family homes, each on half-acre lots with retention ponds and an association run by obviously obsessive residents. She checks the house numbers against the one she wrote down at the library after spending a few minutes Googling directions to her house.

She checks her face in the rearview mirror. It looks swollen from Winthrop's blow, but only modestly so. She touches the tender edges around her eye with light pressure then punches herself once, then again. The car shakes with her violent movements. Her balled left fist brings tears to both eyes.

After collecting herself for a moment, she checks herself again in the rearview mirror. That eye is now roadkill stuck to her face. If Dylan is the protective type, this could persuade her to go with Abby. And by going with her, Abby would be getting it all—tragedy chosen and severe. But if she's the timid type, she might walk Abby out and slam the door in her face as she tries to explain. Either way, Dylan making a decision to go or not go while under this visual duress might nullify the whole feeling. Regardless, Abby can't help but imagine the beauty of going with her.

Abby puts on sunglasses to hide the eye and walks to the door. The dark of the stoop makes her adjust the glasses to find the doorbell. She stands and flips the shoulder strap on her canvas bag over her shoulder. The bag hangs at her side like a dead animal. All that shit from work could have stayed in the car. If she had to have a bag with her, why couldn't it have been that little bag of pot she had squirreled way in her dresser drawer?

Abby jumps as a lock clicks. Then twice more. Dylan holds the door open before her. She's still wearing her work clothes, and despite the look of excitement and confusion on her face, she looks like she's been sitting at a computer all day. "How did you know where I live?"

"I shouldn't have come," Abby says, hoping to bring out the caring side of Dylan.

"No," she says, reaching feebly for Abby. "Come in."

Dylan closes the door behind them, and Abby sets her bag on the ceramic tile. Abby pushes the sunglasses further up her nose with an index finger at each temple. Her hand is still sore, but she wants all the camouflage she can get, for now.

As Dylan shifts her attention, her face contorts in panic, and she dashes out of the room without a word. The sudden burst of energy makes Abby think she just remembered something boiling on the stove.

Looking around, Abby guesses Dylan's either just moved in or didn't fare well in a divorce. The house isn't so much decorated as it is delivered. What there is of it is nice stuff: an assortment of old-fashioned oak pieces positioned around the room, but they're paired with a Scandinavian sofa and coffee table and nothing else. It's like she ordered things by item number in the index at the back of a catalogue instead of by looking at the pictures. The lack of curtains on the windows makes the closed vertical blinds blend into the bare white walls.

When Dylan returns, her face is just as frantic and wide-eyed as when she left the room, but now she has a bag of frozen peas in her outstretched hand. "Put this on your eye for twenty minutes. Then take it off for twenty minutes. We can alternate with a bag of lima beans as we repeat the process. It's the best thing for that. But it will stay black a week to ten days."

Abby removes her sunglasses. She's momentarily speechless that Dylan saw past the sunglasses and knew what to do.

"Have the police been notified?"

"It happened at work. The bouncers got him."

"Why? Why would someone do this to you?"

"He must have been mad about the other day," she says, putting some effort into the illusion of tears.

"Who? Mad about what?"

"I don't want to say."

"Abby? Why? Tell me."

"It was just so humiliating and it hurts so bad." She peeks beneath the bag of peas to see if Dylan's buying it, but she can't be sure.

"Keep the peas on there. Once the inflammation is down, it'll feel better."

Abby snuggles into her a little, hoping she'll hug her back. Instead, Dylan places her hand on Abby's arm, as if for support, but nothing else. Abby worries that she's spoiled her appearance. If Dylan no longer finds her beautiful, her plans could be fucked. She never thought about that.

She makes another crying sound and then says, "You wouldn't think that old bastard could hit so hard. It really hurts."

"Who? What old bastard?"

"Winthrop. Okay? It was Winthrop." Abby stays quiet in order to watch Dylan's face take its natural course. There's shock first, then acknowledgement, then, finally and most deeply, anger.

"If he's actually arrested, he'll make bail by six o'clock," Abby says. "Probably won't even miss work. Most guys like that don't want to draw any attention to themselves after something like that. But, you know..."

"That's it. That little motherfucker has had it."

Abby has nothing else to say. Sitting there, she tilts her head back, absorbs the cold over her sore eye. She's so uncomfortable that she distracts herself with a landscape in oil hanging above the sofa behind Dylan. Through her good eye, this painting is the only color along white walls, white vaulted ceiling, and white built-in bookshelves. No framed mirrors hanging. No pictures behind glass. No shiny surfaces except for the sheen of a freshly polished coffee table. She reaches over and spreads the blinds on the sliding glass doors to see the backyard. No pool, just a couple of tall pines and oaks surrounded by grass and a few large rocks. She closes the blinds and turns to face Dylan again. "Some would say there are no coincidences."

"Fate? That's not likely."

"Well, I'm not talking fate, necessarily. But are you more inclined to believe everything in the world is just random? Don't you take notice of how well it all works and that maybe there's a greater plan we're supposed to ride?"

Seven

As the garage door slides open the next morning, the rollers and springs groan in protest. Ordinarily, Dylan would grab the oilcan and solve the situation, being careful to keep her skirt and blouse clear, but today her urgency precludes such details.

After speeding across the bridge and driving into Clearwater, Dylan parks in the vice president's spot, which she soon learns is six hundred twenty-two steps closer to the side door than her usual spot.

She walks with only her stack of reports under her arm. She leaves her briefcase in the car and today has a hand free to swipe the employee badge to open the door.

The ever-present morning crowd is gathered like socialites around the coffee station, but instead of discussing their mundane activities and the television they watched, their usual bullshit camaraderie, pretend interest, and make-believe friendship, their eyes are downcast, as if the floor is the most interesting thing on earth.

"Winthrop here yet?" Dylan says, poking her head into the break room.

"Haven't you heard?" the overweight receptionist says. Her eyes look up from the floor only for a moment and then pass back down quickly. "Mr. Winthrop passed away last night. Heart failure."

"I never would have suspected he had a heart," Dylan says.

The guy from accounting giggles, but then regains composure.

Some guy from purchasing with a tie that ends near his crotch says, "None of us really liked the guy, but it's rough when one of your own dies. You know?"

"I'm glad he's dead," Dylan says and turns to walk away.

"Sure, because you might finally get his job now."

Dylan clenches her fists, pissed she doesn't get to beat the shit out of Winthrop. "Not me," she says. "Now if you'll excuse me, I've got some files to clean up."

As she sets down the stack of reports on her Formica desktop, she looks at the artificial fish tank. Plastic fish float in blue food coloring with a picture of the sea glued from the back. The metaphor is all too fucking familiar. Leaning her elbows over the back of her chair, she enters her login (mother) and password (fucker) into her computer then plugs in her thumb drive. For the first time, the action is like sinking a key into the ignition of a Ferrari. A surge of adrenaline flushes through her as she selects both the C-drive and the G-drive. Instantly, the file names highlight in muted yellow on the screen. Dylan then deletes all her files and those backed up, locally and on both redundant remotes on the cloud. If the Eidolon Corporation wants any of the research she's done during Winthrop's tenure, they'll have to go back to the old data storage tapes and decipher file names she coded herself. Fuck them. Twenty thousand man-hours and hundreds of reports on multi-million-dollar deals are now digital dust. She has the same feeling of lightness in her chest and torso she had at the end of her enlistment.

She then reaches over the desk and unplugs the faux fish tank and picks it up from the shelf by palming the top of it like a basketball and walks out of her cubicle with the tank's power cord trailing behind until she reaches Benny Sloat's cubicle.

Benny looks up, obviously startled by the surprise visitor.

Dylan hands him the fish tank. "They don't eat much."

Benny's face has that confused creaminess to it. That look of, *You're giving me a gift?* Instead, he says, "Thanks. I think."

"Good luck, handsome." Dylan nods at him, turns to the exit, grabs her employee badge from her back pocket, and tosses it at the trash can.

At Abby's house that morning, there is no sense in trying to hide it. Lawton looks up at her as she slides the sunglasses off.

"I'll kill that fucking cutter."

Abby waves the glasses at him. "It's not her."

"Who then?"

"It's no big deal. It was at work." She takes him by the shoulders and forces him back to his seat. "It's no big deal." But she couldn't have planned it any better.

"That son of a bitch Rifley?"

"Customer. Some random suit," she lies. "A broker or lawyer."

"Did the bouncers get the motherfucker?"

"Yeah, and they were a lot rougher on him than either of us could be. Trust me."

"You sure you're okay?"

"Absolutely."

She opens a beer, hands it to Lawton, and then opens herself one.

"Good news, bro." She lifts her arms off his shoulders flips her hair. She kisses his cheek and says, "You won't have to clean up after me anymore."

"You're finally going to jettison the excess? Unclutter your life? Actually start putting things away for a change?"

"Something like that." Her laughter is more grounded in surprise than mockery. "I'm going on another trip. A long trip."

"Already?" Lawton's cynicism is so adorable. "You're shitting me."

"I wouldn't shit you, Lawton. You're my favorite turd."

"Where are you going this time? And more importantly, with whom are you going?" He leans in pressing and urgent, like the bad cop in an interrogation. She knows he knows the answer to the last question. Knows it's Dylan.

Abby points at him, as if aiming a gun at his face. "You sound like Mother when you talk like that." She fires her finger-gun. "Besides, it's none of your business."

"You're going with that psychotic dyke, aren't you?"

"Dylan's no psycho. She's just a little different." Abby slides herself back, creating more physical distance. "And don't use that term ever again."

"Come on, Ab. You know what I mean. That fucking woman is unstable at best. First the bloodbath then that zombie episode." He lists them off on his fingers. "Besides," he says, "the farther you go and the longer you stay, the more you'll have to risk these black eyes to pay the bills and replenish your bank account."

Abby's face changes. She reaches into her back pocket.

"What are you doing?" Lawton asks.

"I have a list of shit to do." She unfolds an onionskin piece of paper she tore from the back of one of her dictionaries weeks ago. The page is even more wrinkled now from folding and unfolding, and the items are listed in several different colors of ink. "Look at that," she says. "The favor I need from you is first on the list."

They motor down the same stretch of highway Abby drives to Rifley's, but it's a vastly different route in her Jetta with Lawton driving. The stretch of Park Boulevard to the interstate is heavily congested. Even on the other side of the evening rush hour, commuters and snowbirds are a dangerous combination, as are the high speeds and stoplights, and Lawton's tailgating. He rolls within inches of every car in front of him at the lights. After five or six such near misses, he says, "Your handling is weak. You're low on power steering fluid, and the brakes suck, but it beats the shit out of my truck. And by the way, are you sure you want them to see you like this?"

"A black eye won't alter their opinion of me much."

On I-275, the stretch into Tampa is as effortless as the wind through the windows. On the bridge, just before the hump, the pinks and grays in the sky give the horizon a tie-dyed effect.

He keeps his eyes on the road. "Are you sure though?" He doesn't turn his head to watch her nod.

Lawton floors it over the bridge and gears down to take the off-ramp at Howard Avenue, just two exits before Rifley's exit.

On Bayshore Boulevard, the palm-lined sidewalk with its ivory white balustrade extends for six miles along the road Abby grew up on. Street traffic is light there, and mostly dog walkers and joggers pass the old-money houses on the western side of Hillsborough Bay.

As a kid, she'd go there to walk, to watch sunsets and storms roll in, and she thought about the world beyond the horizon that remains unchanged today. In the background, the university's minarets remind her of the old hotel that it used to be. She had such fantasies as a kid lying in her yard in the shadow of history, pretending to know how the world worked in 1900.

She'd watched Lawton play football in the grass median that separates passing traffic.

The looming structure of the hospital just over the water. Sometimes, she secretly hoped he'd get hurt so she could go to the emergency room with him. More often, though, her brother would fish. And though fishing wasn't proper behavior for a young lady, she did it anyway. She'd spent her free time as a child sitting on benches reading. Manatee frequented the shallow waters, and in June she could look up and see tarpon jumping in the distance.

The smell of low tide wafts into the car's open windows as she flips up the visor as they roll along an extensive driveway of intricate brickwork that rises at a gradual incline and runs through sprawling manicured gardens, culminating in a roundabout with a giant fountain in front of the house they grew up in.

All those years living in that house, they were never allowed to park in the driveway. Not even for short periods of time. Mother wouldn't allow it. She reserved the entry for guests. Instead, she made her children enter from the rear, like the housekeeping staff and caterers. Abby always hated having to drive around the house in that loop of masonry brilliance and park in one of the five spots in their garage. Every time she rounded that corner, heading in that direction, she'd see the helicopter pad their father had installed in the back of the property. Pompous ass. She hated being the kid in school with a helicopter. She never even got to ride in it. "It's not a toy," her father had said. "It's simply a conveyance." Like a ten-year-old can comprehend that. So instead of having fun, she got teased about being the rich kid. Since she's been a visitor here these last few trips, she doesn't even go near the garage.

Lawton parks perpendicular to the fountain and kills the engine. "This place is still landscaped to the balls."

Abby isn't in the mood for small talk. "Just have my back if they get on top of me."

"Done." Lawton flashes his war face.

When they ring the bell, she's surprised Mother answers the door herself. Despite the early evening hour, Abby hoped the housekeeper would still be there.

"Well, Lord have mercy. You're just as cute as kittens." Their mother is all veneered-teeth smiles. Her rings are wrapped around a highball glass with less ice than scotch. Abby doesn't know if this is drink one, two, or three into cocktail hour. "Lawton, how cute," she says. "You always dress like you're coming from work."

Lawton clears his throat and stretches his neck without speaking.

"Oh, where are my manners? Please, get in here, you two." Their mother opens the door wide and sweeps the air with her free hand.

She's wearing her patented silk "house clothes" and her Manolo Blahniks. Funny how silk and expensive shoes of any kind can be appropriate for any occasion.

Mother reaches out to hug them simultaneously.

Abby crosses her arms, covers her nipples as she stands there. "Why do you have to keep it like a meat freezer in here?"

Lawton dips a shoulder in a little and Mother pats his back. Hugs always seemed awkward and no one had ever shown interest in practicing. Firm handshakes always served the purpose. Protocol at the Stratton household.

"Your father's on a conference call, but he'll be out to join us momentarily."

The old man couldn't set aside business for anything.

"I'm sorry for the short notice," Abby says, removing her sunglasses.

Mother closes the door behind them as they face the foyer. "Don't be silly, darling. It was a thrill to get your call." She takes Abby's hand in hers. "You know how I love pleasant surprises. Oh my god, is that a black eye?"

"It was just an accident at the restaurant where I work," she lies. "It's no big deal."

"But it must be so painful."

"I filed with worker's comp," she lies again.

"Well, that's a wise thing, I suppose." Mother leads them through the foyer into the living room, the room where Abby and Lawton spent most of their time as kids. It still seems big now—this single room is bigger than the house Lawton and Abby live in—but nothing in the room looks familiar. Furnishings and décor change every three years or so. Mother has a way of redecorating or updating or modernizing or whatever other euphemism she uses to deny her need to spend. Her lack of sentimentality.

But every item in the room looks as if it belongs. It always does. It's like different pieces making the same puzzle. All the same basic superfluous shit but in different colors, textures, and styles. Looking around the room, the stuff surrounding her is on a countdown to becoming obsolete as far as Mother is concerned.

Abby walks to the wall of windows.

Situated on six acres, the view of the bay extends to two

hundred seventy degrees, every inch viewable through twenty-two-foot arched windows separated by French doors leading onto tiled balconies. The water still captures her imagination. But now they have high-rise condo buildings on the banks across from them, the horizon in the distance obscured. Of all the things Abby misses from her childhood home, it is the bay. That fat belly of water that carries yachts and barges and flows hot into untold oceans and majestic seas. It is days spent out there reading, listening to feeble waves breaking on the bank, buoy bells and boat horns echoing in the air that Abby misses most.

She feels a tap on her shoulder.

"Mother asked you if you'd care for a beverage," Lawton says.

"I'll have whatever you're having."

"New drapes?" Lawton points with his chin as she makes the drinks for him and Abby.

Their mother shakes her head and says, "What's keeping your father?" She walks toward the grand hall leading to his study. "Oh, here he comes."

The patriarch of the dysfunctional family strides with the gait of a corporate raider even in his own home. His heels clomp the marble floor to announce his entrance. His suit coat is missing, presumably draped over the chair back in his home office. Abby hates her father's pitch-black toupee, the leather suspenders, the clean-shaven face, totally devoid of the five o'clock shadow despite it being past six. When he enters the living room, he kisses their mother, as he always does upon greeting her. They embrace effortlessly as he leans forward and she reaches up. They kiss again.

"That was the police following up on the dead deer out at the eastern property."

Abby's mother produces a compact and checks her lipstick. "Have they any new information?"

"The initial responders fouled up any chances to get usable footprints, but the cleaning crew found three marijuana seeds on the bunk room floor. I don't suppose you two would know anything about this?"

"Don't point fingers at us. We haven't even eaten meat in three years," Lawton says.

Their father fidgets with his gold cufflinks before thrusting out a hand for his son to shake. "Lawton. Good to see you." He waves his other hand to signify Lawton's clothes. "Sorry if this meeting had to pull you out in the middle of your work."

Lawton squeezes his father's hand tighter. "Clothes don't make the man, Father."

Their father releases his grip. "Don't get me started." He turns an about-face and greets Abby with the same courteous manner. "Abigail." He holds out that same right hand. "It's always a pleasure to see you. You're looking well, despite that shiner."

"Father." Abby shakes his hand. "Thank you for taking the time to see us on such short notice. And this is nothing," she says, patting the bone under her eye. Abby knows she won't have to explain it because she catches Mother out of the corner of her eye, signaling for him to drop the topic.

"I'm glad our schedules meshed," he says, then checks his watch before waving off the attempted sarcasm with a faint curl of his lip. His attempt at a smile.

"Don't be silly. Our house is your house," Mother says, patting Abby's shoulder.

Abby rolls her eyes. How dare they schmooze their own daughter.

"Well." Mother drinks from her scotch as she walks to the couch closest to the French doors. "Why don't we all sit and have a nice visit."

The fumes from new paint, new rugs, and drapes assault Abby's nostrils. That smell will stay with her awhile, the artificial scent. It's just a little fresher than the smell in funeral homes. Here the smell blends nicely with their artificial lives. The fresh flowers on the center of every table emit no scent.

"The suspense is just killing me." Mother pats down the back of her overly blonde hair. "What is the occasion for this lovely visit?" She slaps her thigh with her hand. "Have you two decided to go to graduate school?"

Father strains a mixing tin of chilled gin into a martini glass and adds cocktail onions imported from Spain. "MBAs would catch you two right up. Get you back in the game," he says.

"No. No." Abby sets her drink on a coaster. "Nothing that dramatic." She looks at Lawton. "I've just come to say goodbye and Lawton wanted to come along." Abby hates the lie.

"Goodbye?" Their father takes a seat opposite his wife. "Where are you going?"

Mother sits up. Excitement pulls her features into a Botox- and collagen-injected smile. "Are you going to Austria to continue your piano playing?"

Piano. Those days were behind her. She'd changed since playing on scheduled events with all her parent's over-appreciative friends in attendance, where afterward Abby had to talk to the old men and ladies who'd held martinis and chanted, "Bravo."

Abby looks at Lawton. They both laugh. Abby wonders what else she's on, besides scotch.

"No, Mother." Abby scoots to the edge of the sofa cushion. "I'm going on a trip. A very long trip with a friend of mine."

"One of your adult entertainer friends?" Father sucks an onion off a little sword. He changes hands with his glass.

"Don't start that," Abby says.

"You'll both be turning thirty next week. It's time you both grew up and took on some responsibility for once in your life. I didn't build everything I have to turn it over to strangers for Christ's sake."

"Ah, the big three-oh," Mother says, setting down her drink. "It's right around the corner." She scoots to the edge of the sofa. "Won't you let me throw you a party?"

Abby points to Lawton. "I can't speak for him, but if you want a party, throw a damn party. I won't be here."

"Oh, you're so cruel," Mother says, grabbing her drink as she slides back and crosses her legs. "There's no need to be like that. You're just upset about the milestone. But don't be."

"I'm not."

"It's only natural."

"You have no idea what's natural."

"What's that supposed to mean?"

"Forget it."

Her father interrupts. "If we could focus on the real matter at hand, ladies."

Abby retreats to a neutral corner, not because her father demanded it, but because she no longer cares to discuss it.

"Fine," Father says. "Then let's drop the pretenses and just tell us why you're living like you do. Why don't you use the money in your trust and straighten out your lives?"

Abby picks up the first thing within her reach. It's a hand-painted porcelain candy dish her mother bought in Paris on their honeymoon. "Not another fucking word about that goddamn trust!" The candy dish sails across the room, farther than Abby would have thought, and crashes into the wall above the credenza, barely missing the gilded mirror hanging there. Fragments of porcelain rain down heavy.

"That's not necessary," Father says.

"We can talk like civil adults, can we not?" Mother says, trying to ignore the mess.

Abby looks for something else to throw, but instead alights upon the rack of fireplace tools. "Well," she says, sidestepping closer to the fireplace while looking into the far corner of the room. "I don't know." She picks up the shovel by mistake and replaces it, instead selects the iron poker. The weight of it in her hands surprises her. Looking at her mother, Abby curls the iron like a weightlifter, then swings it through the air like a golf club. "You still hitting the links, Mother?"

"Well, I've been so busy around here. I'm lucky to get out there once a week."

"Pity," Abby says. She then swings the iron poker down onto the coffee table, where the hook end catches into the wood.

"Abigail Vaughn Stratton!" Mother stands, hands on her hips. "That's enough."

"Honestly, child. What's gotten into you? Is it drugs?" Father looks over at Lawton. "Are you two methed up right now? Is that it?"

"There's no drugs, you ass," Abby says.

"Then what is this all about?"

"I just wanted to say goodbye." Abby pries the iron poker free from the coffee table and throws it javelin style, through the seventy-inch television screen. "So, goodbye."

Lawton takes the hint. He lunges out of his seat and toward the foyer. Opening the door, he looks back and waves at his parents. "Take it easy," he says, letting Abby out and closing the door behind them.

Back in Abby's Jetta, she watches the headlights reflect off the driveway pavers as Lawton heads out. She wants to get the hell out of there, but he rolls to a stop before reaching the road.

"Whatever you're up to, I'm against it," he says, tears obscured by shadows.

"I know. But I'm going to do it."

"I don't want you to."

"It's not your place to say."

"I can't let you do something so…"

"So what? So stupid?"

"I didn't say that."

"Oh, fuck this. This is just so fucking cliché."

"Look. I can't help it, okay? Think if this shit was reversed."

Abby gets it then. Obligation tugs against her chest. "Okay. Don't think of it as the last time you'll ever see me, but more like the first day of my eternal happiness."

"And Dylan?" he asks, wiping his cheek with his shoulder.

"What about her?"

"You're taking her with you?"

"We're kind of taking each other," she says, still looking straight ahead.

"That's murder."

"She's old enough to make her own decisions."

"Are you?"

"Dude, come on." She looks over at him, raises her index finger. "This is the one thing I want."

"Why can't you be this adamant about living?"

"Then I wouldn't be me, now would I?"

Lawton shifts the car into gear and pulls out.

Once on the open road, he restricts his speed. Seeing their parents usually gives him an edge, a bitter shot of adrenaline, but he isn't in the mood to test the car's performance now.

Abby reclines the passenger seat, angles it back a few inches.

Lawton pinches the bottom of the wheel and reaches his free hand over to pat her knee. "I'm not going to stop you...even though I want to."

He can't. Doing so would prove him every bit the fucking hypocrite their parents are. Abby lolls her head to look at him. "I know that."

There's nothing he can do.

She is free.

Silk skirts and oxford-cloth shirts sustain a fire longer than Dylan ever imagined. And though the campfire she lit in her backyard flames just fine, she stokes the fire with another pair of black pumps and recoils at the toxic smell of chemicals and charred tree branches. Around the fire and around her feet are scattered items she'd dropped in piles after running to and from the house to get more stuff to burn. The more she burns, the more she wants to burn. She'd like to feed the fire everything she has. Simplify her life without this shit. Sure she answered to the

Corps while she served, but when you were good at your job, the Corps asked little else of you than to keep up the good work. She'd gotten out with nothing but a car, a seabag, stellar evaluations, and a checking account with nine hundred dollars.

Except for the faint oxygen swish of the fire and the acceleration of an occasional car passing over Mill Road in the distance, Dylan's backyard is completely quiet. Crickets or cicadas or whatever entomologists call them crank in the grass all around her. This white noise is the same as the buzz of human voices in the office...except when Winthrop blasted somebody. And fuck him, anyway. Dylan hated that the dirty bastard died before she could get her hands on him.

The yard is on a conservation lot that is like Black Forest acreage to Dylan now and no one can see her. In total privacy, she piles more pages of reports, then another pair of pumps and a work blouse. This span of time at the fire is already the longest she's spent in her own yard in as long as she can remember. Dylan flips the last work skirt into the fire with a stick and spits into the flames at the thought of any kind of lawsuit that might drop from the homeowners association. She leans in, feels the heat rising from the small fire in her yard. It flushes her face like embarrassment once did. She feels herself redden, absorbing the fire. Contained arson, of sorts. One errant spark, one wayward flame, and this house, this subdivision, the whole drought-plagued county would be reduced to ashes and charred memories.

As the flames heat her face, the midmorning sun warms her back and a column of smoke rises through the canopy of leaves and branches overhead. She makes a mental note to learn the trees' names and species.

The conservation area directly behind her house is crowded with trees and she doesn't know what any of them are—oaks maybe, or some sort of elms perhaps. Inhaling the smoke as it mixes with the scent of gardenia growing wild in the bushes on the far side of her yard, she sits all the way back into her dusty folding beach chair. The yard work has long been delegated to a man she's never met who maintains most of the subdivision. A guy Dylan mails a check to every month, but never sees. That guy spends more time taking care of these bushes and this yard in one afternoon than Dylan's spent out here since she's owned the place.

Even with the smoke rising off the burned remnants of her everyday mistakes, she's enjoying the grass—that fresh scent of chlorophyll immolates her baggage of misguided energy, the misspent years. Nothing has ever given her more pleasure, but as she watches their symbols blacken to ash, she shifts in her seat. Uncomfortable. She decides then that she'll get a nicer chair in which to spend time enjoying the yard. Maybe an Adirondack chair. Maybe she'll go all out and get a hammock. Either would be good. More comfortable than this rusty old beach chair that hasn't touched sand since Clinton held office.

It isn't yet noon, but she's liberated, feels like an asylum escapee. Instead of a straitjacket or hospital gown, she folds a suit coat into the fire. She has a metal garbage can filled with the detritus from her desk and the articles of the corporate uniform she's been obligated to wear these past many years. She feels reborn. Resurrected. Immortal. Worshipable.

The fire burns strong, but she rips off ten pages at a time from the report she's been working on and feeds the fire. As each page ignites, flames lick the edges, curling and then browning them before making their way up to the body of each sheet of paper, devouring them completely.

There exists a bizarre pleasure in watching the numbers she spent so much time accumulating disappear in a hiss of heat and oxygen. There is nothing to do but watch. There is such sensuality in the way they turn to ash, most of which falls to the bottom while other flakes of it fly away. There had been none of that emotion in their creation.

This thought goes on until a plane, deviating from the regular flight path, flies over the house. The reverberation of its engines echoes in her ribs. There are sixty-one thousand people flying over the US at any given hour. Traveling. Seeing. Doing. Business or pleasure, those lucky bastards all get a change of scenery. Off their wheels. Out of their cages. She envies their freedom before realizing freedom is what she now has.

There's no way she can go back to corporate hell, that white-collar concentration camp, that cemetery called headquarters. Cubical walls and headstones are the same thing to her. Going to work every day, fifty weeks a year, got her no closer to her dreams of fulfillment than masturbating got her nearer to marrying a movie star. There's no point in continuing. She's had enough of the office life, with its voice mail conversations and vending machine meals. That fucking never-empty inbox. Office politics, team building bullshit. Cost analysis, cost prohibitive. Feasibility studies. The Seven Habits of Clock Watchers, wage slaves, the terminally in debt who inch their way to a retirement they'll be too ill to enjoy. Ill from a lifetime of inactivity and bad habits, the result of too much work, too much spending, too many bills, and too much stress. As long as their health plan covers it, why bother trying to prevent it? Suckers. The hell with long commutes, road rage, talk radio. She's tired of life as a rodent, trapped in a cage with piss-saturated wood chips. She's had enough of spinning incessantly on the corporate wheel, expending energy, going nowhere. The planet will rotate if she doesn't show up at her desk on Tuesday morning. The world's economy won't even hiccup if her quarterly report isn't completed. She's never allowed herself time to pursue romance, and therefore, has no significant other, no girlfriends, no boy-friends. No meaningful relationships of any kind. No pets. No friends. No hobbies. No creative absorptions to immerse herself in. Her vacations are spent alone, working, from home. Catching up. Getting ahead. Always working, never living. She lobs another suit coat onto the fire as she thinks of Abby.

Now, now she has Abby...and this little fire at her feet.

* * *

Abby walks through Dylan's house and finds her in the backyard poking a little bonfire with a stick. "Isn't it a little warm for a campfire? And early?" Before Dylan can answer, Abby looks to the piles of papers, clothes, and office supplies. "Seriously, I'm glad you're home. I was worried you might've gotten arrested."

"For what?"

"How bad did you rough up Winthrop?"

"He's dead," Dylan says. "Let's leave it at that."

"Oh my god." Abby covers her nose as a plastic three-ring binder flares in the fire. She's pleased to know Dylan can be ruthless in her vengeance. But as she watches her throw another report onto the fire, Abby has no way of knowing Dylan's full potential. It didn't really matter. Yet. "So what's with the burning?"

"I'm done." Dylan tosses papers and a stapler into the fire. "I want out. This is me, getting all the way out."

For a moment it's like a choir appears through the bolts of sunshine and sings "Hallelujah."

"Really?" Abby says.

"I don't know." Dylan clasps her hands behind her head and pumps her elbows together hard enough to click. "I'm just losing it today," she says through arms crossed over her head.

Abby feels tension rise out of her like a cloud, all at once. "Maybe it's the opposite," she says, bending to pick up a stack of Post-its. "Maybe you're getting something now." She extends her arm over the fire and chucks the Post-its into the center. Sparks fly and embers jump. "Bigger and better things. And now you're finally able to go in search of what that might be."

"You mean unemployment."

"Stop that negative shit. Think about the possibilities, the endless fucking possibilities. You know? Fuck the old. Go with what's new." She circles the fire as Dylan adds a handful of stockings and three, thick manila folders.

Abby snugs up on Dylan from behind. She works her hands over Dylan's shoulders and down her arms to her hands to her hips, where she massages her fingers closer to her crotch. But just before she gets there, she nibbles on Dylan's ear and says, "You'll need a bigger fire to get you all the way out."

Dylan twists her head as Abby pushes away from her. "A lot bigger fire."

Abby squeezes the container of lighter fluid to arc into the center of the fire. Flames shoot up toward the tree branches; a billow of smoke engulfs them. "Hey," Dylan calls out, "be careful."

The can in Abby's hands is almost full. "Do you want all the way out?"

Dylan looks to the ground for a moment, then back up to Abby. They hold eye contact long enough for Abby to record the connection in her memory. Dylan nods, looks to the sky, and says, "Yes."

Moments later, the flames reach and ignite a branch overhead, which becomes a torch to light the eaves of Dylan's roof like a fuse.

"Oh, fuck," Dylan says, running to the hose on the other side of the screen-covered lanai.

Abby chases her, stops her from turning on the spigot. "Wait a minute," she says, her hand on Dylan's, caressing her way up to her shoulder and then turning Dylan around to face her.

Dylan squirms beneath Abby's grip while staring at the flames. "You want me to just watch it burn?"

"It's all just stuff," Abby says. "You want all the way out, right?"

Through a panicked expression that isn't attractive to Abby, Dylan says, "I spent years saving for the down payment."

"You're insured. And you've got time to grab the essentials...if you hurry."

As Dylan turns to go inside, Abby worries she might try to barricade herself in there and go out like some sort of martyr.

"I'll go with you," Abby says, with the realization that it will save them time and trouble if they perish in there together. "Let's go."

The smoke detectors throughout the house ring salvos in urgent repeated beeps. Dylan holds her breath and darts from room to room, picking up a paperweight from her desk and then a little metal box from the closet before running back to her bedroom. She keeps fire extinguishers in the kitchen and garage, but they're useless against flames this size. With dense smoke filling the top two-thirds of the room, Dylan crawls into her bathroom and takes as clean a breath as she can get, hoping it will hold her until she gets outside.

As she double-checks the inventory in her shower kit, she finds the X-ACTO knife. The searing blade had slipped her mind until now. The shining blade is a welcome back sign that's more nostalgic than inviting. She considers its weight it in her hand, the simple design. The delicate crosshatch of the knurling in the handle is familiar to her fingers, but gone is the raw power it once possessed. Gone is the perverse pleasure of holding a knife. It's something different. Now, there is no temptation despite the energy flowing through her and it seems easy. She's been reprogrammed, chemically altered through the hormones of...what? Happiness? Something better? It's so much better with Abby.

The incessant beeping of the smoke detectors dwindles, and she imagines the flames licking high enough to burn out the alarms in the kitchen and hall. The one that still works is just above her bedroom door and it grates on her. As she holds her breath, she stuffs the shower kit into her backpack, and as she grabs a couple of pairs of underwear and the one pair of jeans remaining there, she is forced to cover her mouth and nose with a plain white T-shirt as she drops to her knees and crawls out. All but one item she wants fits into the backpack. She runs out to the living room and tosses the bag to Abby before taking a huge breath and running back into the bedroom to crawl her way back to finding the one item she really wants.

They make it out of the house in time to hear fire trucks barreling down 56th Street from Busch Boulevard. Dylan coughs from the smoke in her last inhalation in the house, and shivers from the temperature difference in the outside air. She didn't realize how close to the flames she must have been.

In the driveway, Abby drops the backpack at her feet while Dylan sets a sewing form between them. It's a little darker from the smoke and maybe some ash, but she's got it.

"A backpack and that. That's all you're taking?"

The question seems obvious to her. "Of course." For years, the sewing form has been a comforting figure standing there in the corner of her room. "I can't leave her."

"Seriously? There's nothing in there you want more than that dummy?"

"This is all I need, and it's not a dummy."

"Please tell me you don't make dresses in your spare time."

"It's my mother."

"Okay. I'm not the judgmental kind. I'll just assume it's some ironic sort of objet d'art. Very postmodern." By now smoke wafts through the eaves and higher into the trees. "We'd better go. Take that thing if you want to."

Fire trucks pull up at that moment, and in a flash of reflective tape and fire hoses, a number of men in Nomex suits charge the fire hydrant near the sidewalk. Others storm the house with other hoses. Abby pulls Dylan out of the way, but the sewing form is left to get trampled by a hurried boot on the way to battle roof-high flames. The stand snaps as two overlapped fire hoses charge. As the torso lies in the driveway, a firefighter kicks it on his way into the house. It all happens in surreal cinematography. Among the blurring edges of Dylan's periphery, her neighbors shout her name and someone calls for the keys to the car in the garage, but Dylan watches the body of the cleaving sewing form.

A piece of Dylan breaks off right there, as if she were also made of cardboard. Seeing it like that leaves nerve endings raw and electric, like her entire body is the socket of a knocked-out tooth. All those years, she never considered it hollow, and seeing it like that proves just how empty her life has been. Before Abby, Dylan never felt so important or wanted, and she would never have considered watching her house burn without Abby. Since meeting her, Dylan feels connected in ways she never could have predicted.

Abby tugs Dylan's arm and says, "We better get out of here before it gets complicated."

The house is ablaze and has hoses streaming through broken windows, a dozen men trotting in and around. She knows full well what she's doing is wrong, but she doesn't dare equivocate in Abby's presence. A knot throbs in the pit of her stomach reminding her that Abby is bad news. But more prevalent is the centrifugal pressure that keeps Dylan's negative thoughts pinned to her cranium instead of circulating through her brain.

A brass fitting that connects two shorter hoses streams enough water to darken the sun-drenched driveway in front of the house. Water arcs just high and far enough to splash onto the dress form. Cardboard absorbs water between the fibers and grows dense. It is now muddy paste.

"Fuck it," Dylan says. "Let's get out of here."

Eight

In the car, Abby watches smoke billow in the rearview mirror, her eyes shifting to make sure they aren't being followed or chased. Relief is an exhale that relaxes her facial muscles and allows her to breathe more deeply. After making a turn at the stop sign, she says to Dylan, "Now you have to come stay with me."

"Don't take this the wrong way, but I'm not going anywhere near your brother."

"Is there a *right* way to take that?"

"I guess not. No."

Abby doesn't know what to say immediately. Things had moved so quickly. It's understandable that Dylan doesn't want anything to do with Lawton, but Abby's momentarily strapped for options. She steers with her knee and digs her phone out of her bag, then dials. "Dejah, it's me. Can you put me and a friend up for the night?"

"Of course," Dejah says without hesitation. "I hope he's someone we can share."

"It's a she," Abby says. She hadn't thought of that, but now that it's been mentioned, any girl letting go of her job and her house for her deserved such a reward. "And, yeah. Absolutely. And you know what? You better prepare yourself. She's something else."

"Rack her up," Dejah says. "Oh, wait. Is it the girl from the other night?"

"None other."

"Your timing couldn't be better. I'm horny as hell and I've got the next two days free."

"I like the sound of that," Abby says. And she does. But when she hangs up, she makes a U-turn at the next light.

Those few seconds on the phone with Dejah were all the time she needed to consider the potential ramifications of sharing Dylan—not because of affection or any sense of propriety, but because she needs Dylan's full attention. She's made a couple major disconnects in a very short span of time. If she's going to bring Dylan completely onboard, she needs to do so strategically. And as enjoyable as a couple days with Dejah might be for all of them, it just wouldn't help cement her plan. She takes Interstate 75 south and keeps driving.

"Where are we going?" Dylan says, as Abby veers right toward the northbound I-275 exit.

She knows Dylan well enough to know that if she doesn't answer her, she won't ask again. So Abby waits until they approach the tollbooth at the foot of the Sunshine Skyway Bridge connecting the greater reaches of Tampa Bay. "I told you," she says. "We're going to the beach."

"No, you didn't.'

"I meant that by wanting to see the sunset."

"I thought we were going to your friend's place."

"I'm in the mood for some sand between my toes. Just you and me and the sunset."

Two tollbooths later they make it into St. Pete Beach, where the sky is a milky swirl of pinks and creams. It's that ambiguous time when Abby wouldn't know if it's just getting light or just getting dark. It's her favorite time of day to wake up, and she's happy now heading into it with Dylan.

Abby pulls into the parking lot of an orange stucco beachside hotel, and without checking in, they walk around back and right onto the beach. Dylan is a little hesitant to follow, and while Abby ditches her shoes where the sidewalk opens to sand, Dylan keeps hers on and lumbers through the sugar sand.

Abby grabs Dylan's hand. She loves the salty Gulf air hanging all around them. She last witnessed a sunset on this same stretch of beach with the girl before Vince. A petite chick named Annika who she recalls had mild eye twitches and a habit of always being on broadcast—she never shut up and never let Abby explain anything. She didn't keep Annika around for more than four days. But Dylan is different. While Abby pads and splashes at the surf's edge, Dylan walks just out of reach of the mildly rolling water.

The familiar tickle in the back of Abby's throat is from the islands of algae blooms, and plankton scattered in the near-calm Gulf water catch her attention. She coughs and says to Dylan, "Red tide."

The beach is empty except for dead fish and the hollowed carcasses of horseshoe crabs lining the water's edge on either side of the hotel. Up ahead a man in coveralls digs holes with a fast shovel and buries everything on the hotel's beachfront.

Dylan coughs once from the invisible gases in the air, and it reminds Abby of the first time Dylan hit the joint, back at the hunting shed. Abby can only hope that such a laughing fit is on its way because Dylan looks so sullen. So far, Abby's been able to keep her compliant, and she's fucked her to the point of exhaustion every chance she's gotten, but still, her stomach tightens with paranoia that Dylan will hit her stopping point just like the others before her. Only now, Abby simply has no more time. She has only eight days until her absolute deadline.

She'll continue to reward Dylan, if she continues to perform the tasks that will prove she's the one for the job. "Everything will be okay," she says.

Instead of responding, Dylan walks along with her head down, dodging dead fish carcasses.

After retrieving their bags from the car an hour later, they enter the lobby to check in. The change in temperature crawls up

Dylan's arms, and she's still got a tickle in her throat from exposure to the red tide fungus wafting off the water. But as her eyes transition from the sun to the dim lighting in the lobby, she feels the clerk's discomfort about Abby's black eye. Dylan inhales all the air her lungs will hold and drops her backpack at her feet. It's like being a kid again with her mother in that condition. People stared, some whispered. Now though, conditions being what they are, she can't help wondering if this guy assumes she's responsible for putting the color around Abby's eye. Abby told her at least a dozen times not to worry about it as they walked on the beach, but that's easier to do when she wears her sunglasses. Now, they're pushed up on her head, holding hair out of her face as she takes charge and speaks to the clerk behind the desk.

Dylan pushes her way past Abby at the registration desk, holding her wallet toward the clerk.

Abby pulls her arms back. "I've got it."

"I really think I should," Dylan says.

The way Abby looks at her then reminds her of the look in the deer's eye through the sights of the scope. That same pleading stare. But instead of a weapon, Dylan holds her wallet. Instead of an arrow, she wields a credit card.

"Can I have a word with you?" Abby says, grabbing her by the wrist and guiding her away.

Dylan looks to the clerk, but says nothing.

Outside, beneath the awning covering the entrance, Abby says, "What the hell are you doing?"

"I want to pay."

"You can't use your credit cards. Hello? They'll track you and find you and make you answer questions you don't want to hear right now."

"That's true," Dylan says, folding her wallet into her back pocket.

"And you can't use an ATM either."

Dylan feels trapped. Indentured. Going back would mean, at

the least, detainment, which would take her away from Abby. That might be all the time she needs to get away. There's no way she will risk losing her now.

"So unless you've got a couple thousand dollars in cash tucked in your backpack, I think you should make peace with me paying. I don't mind. Really. It's my pleasure."

After the check-in process, a bellman in matching shorts and shirt wheels their two bags to their room on a brass cart, opens the door and shows them the thermostat, the mini-fridge, and then explains that the door to the balcony cuts off the air conditioner when it's open.

Dylan has a few bills in her hand, but she doesn't know how much to tip the guy. She holds up a dollar and the bellman looks displeased, so Dylan peels off a five and the guy's smile widens. "Enjoy your stay," he says, taking the tip.

As the door closes, Abby says, "I'm going to freshen up." She extracts a pair of high-heel shoes from her bag and disappears into the bathroom. The promise of having sex with her again makes Dylan tingle, and she hopes Abby will come out with the blade again. She hopes, but doesn't dare expect.

A few moments later Abby emerges from the bathroom, nude except for the shoes. She's smiling at Dylan and she has something in her hand.

After joining her on the bed, Abby cuts a new scar-to-be the size of a deck of cards while tonguing Dylan's anus and massaging her clitoris. Dylan is aware of the wetness streaming into Abby's mouth. Abby swipes blood with her finger and mixes the two fluids in her mouth, licking her lips as she swallows. It's more personally intense than anything they've done to that point, and Dylan is too excited by it to do anything but hug her arms around herself and hold her breath.

Cleve Bejeak sits in his chair reading a book about Churchill as the call comes over the police scanner. A house fire mobilized the Temple Terrace fire department. It sounds like a total loss on the house already, but they hoped to keep the fire from spreading to other houses and to keep the locked car in the garage from exploding. Instead of getting up, Cleve adjusts his reading glasses and makes a mental note to look up the incident in the newspaper tomorrow.

St. Pete Beach is a parade in a pressure cooker later that night. Dylan would rather be almost anywhere else. So many people cramming the coast, making a hot place hotter. If there were fewer people maybe some of that gulf breeze could circulate around the place.

It's Friday night and the locals are out in full force, mixing around restaurants and bars with tourists. Dylan is nothing but a tourist. She doesn't belong there. She should be home, but then she thinks of her home—a crime scene.

"Relax," Abby says. "The room is on my card. No one can connect us, and no one will think to look for you here."

Dylan's sure that Abby thinks it's about the money, but Dylan's not doing well being out amongst people accompanied by a woman with a black eye. It's the whole Mom thing, but bigger. Though she's too timid to say something to Abby for fear of insulting her appearance, she can't stop thinking about it.

"Look," Abby says. "I don't care, and it's my eye. It doesn't even involve you." She flashes a slightly condescending smile, but from where Dylan's standing, it shows as certainty.

She's wrong. It does involve her. She feels everyone is looking at them.

In a dented yellow Hyundai that smells like curry and ammonia, right after sunset they make their way to a restaurant that Abby says has the best grouper on the west coast. Her hands roam over

Dylan's legs and up over her breasts. She leans in and kisses her neck.

"Not here, Abby. Come on." Dylan pulls Abby's hands down and together, her inhibition cuffing Abby at the wrist. Abby's eye is still a little discolored, but now it's more yellow than black. "Why didn't we just drive?"

"Because we're getting drunk tonight." Abby endures the new arm position without discomfort and asks, "What's with you?"

"Not in public."

Abby looks around, then back at Dylan. "We're in a car."

"Exactly." Dylan releases Abby's arms and nods at the driver.

Abby points. "What? Him?"

Dylan touches a finger to her lips, then knifes it across her throat, pantomiming the universal expressions for *shush* and the *kill* sign.

Abby still points. "Hey," she hollers. "Driver. Will it offend you if me and my girlfriend smooch it up back here?"

The driver looks at them in his rearview mirror. "Look, man," he says in a Bahamian accent. "Two in the pink and one in the stink, man." He holds up the fingers on his right hand with his thumb holding down the ring finger as he laughs. "As long as you don't be splashing your fluids all over my back seat, you can do what you like." He checks the road and then looks back into the mirror. "Two chicks? Shit, man, I can smell that all night."

"See?" Abby looks at Dylan. "He doesn't mind."

Dylan shakes her head.

Abby eases over to Dylan's side of the car. "What do you care what this guy thinks?"

Dylan leans over and kisses her, square on the mouth. It is the first time she's initiated contact in public. They kiss like high school kids until the car stops at their destination.

Theodore's Pub is exactly as Abby remembered it, except there's a different folk singer playing his guitar in hushed tones in the corner of the restaurant. There are ballads and toasts and they're all so poetic that Abby almost wants to hug the singer. Instead, she dances in her seat.

The place is scattered with tables of spring break vacationers, a few locals, two families, some power couples, and, over toward the back, a table of six college kids, their eruptions of laughter drawing attention from the manager by the front door.

A waitress in a mini-kilt and knee socks stops by their table and Abby orders them both blackened grouper sandwiches and a Guinness for herself, then sits back and watches Dylan ask for a glass of hot water.

The waitress asks, "You want tea, ma'am?"

"No. Just a tall glass of really hot water."

"She'll take a Pepsi, too," Abby says.

When the drinks are delivered, Dylan places her silverware into the glass of hot water. One at a time: fork, knife, spoon. Then, after a moment, she extracts the spoon and wipes it in her napkin. Then the knife. Saving the fork for last. Abby wonders if the order has some significance.

The waitress offers to bring Dylan another set of silverware.

Dylan waves her off saying, "Don't trouble yourself."

Abby puts down her menu. She's excited they're here, and anxious to know if she can set the hook deep enough before Dylan wants to run away, like the others. "Cheers," she says, holding up her beer.

Dylan holds up her Pepsi, not for the cheers, but instead holding it to the light and rotating it.

"What are you doing?"

"I'm not sure this glass has been cleaned properly."

"Let me see," Abby says, reaching for the glass. Once she has it in her possession, she bends forward with her tongue fully extended and licks the rim of the glass. She twirls the glass all the way around, licking it as if it were an ice cream cone, and hands it back to Dylan. "There you go. Now the only germs on it are mine."

Dylan looks down to the menu open before her. "This place is pricey."

Abby wedges her foot in Dylan's crotch and massages her with gentle toes. "We're not worrying about money. It's on me, remember?"

"Right."

Their table sits beneath a mounted fishing net. There's scuba gear to their right, where two guys apparently notice Abby's foot in Dylan's crotch and make catcalls. Abby ignores them at first, but they persist in making comments about her foot.

"They're getting themselves warmed up for us," one of them says.

"You girls want to go have a real party?" the other one hollers.

Abby laughs at the lack of subtlety, and their ignorance.

Dylan's face is red and her fists are on the table, elbows wide. Through clenched teeth, she says, "Excuse me a minute."

Abby finds it a strange time for Dylan to go to the restroom, but instead Dylan walks directly to their table.

One guy has a frying pan for a nose and the other guy is chewing too big a bite. As Dylan walks over to their table, the guy with the frying pan nose says, "And what do you think you're going to do?"

Abby's tempted to stop her—they don't need any trouble with the police—but she's curious what Dylan might actually be capable of. She watches Dylan's profile. She smiles at their leathery faces, leans down, and places her hands flat on the table. A fork is inches from her right hand. Abby wonders if Dylan will pick it up and stab it into the guy's carotid artery and watch him bleed out. Instead, Dylan coughs once and then grabs the pan-nose guy by the throat, catching him with food that can go neither down nor out and his eyes go round as golf balls.

With Dylan's khaki pants and polo shirt, people might come to conclusions about her sexuality, but there's no way anyone could guess she had these kinds of skills.

"This is the tracheal twist," Dylan says, inches from the guy's face. Her back flares out wide enough to stretch her pink shirt. "It's the most immediate weapon in hand-to-hand combat." The other guy scrambles to get up, but Dylan thrusts out a leg to block his path. "Stay seated or your friend will never sound the same." Turning her attention back to the matter at hand, she says, "I push a little harder into your doughy fucking throat, I'll be able to wrap my hand around your entire tracheal. You know what I'm saying?" Dylan then looks over to the other guy, who is sitting still, giving her his undivided attention. She says to them both, "With as much energy as it takes to yawn, I can rip this fucking thing clean out of your neck and watch you drop, wide-eyed and freaked out, onto the table."

"We're sorry," the other guy says without moving. "Let him go. We're sorry."

"I'd like to remain strangers," Dylan says. "You know what I mean?"

"You got it. Just let him go."

"You're sorry?" Dylan says into the guy's panicked face.

The guy can't chew and can't swallow, and when he tries to answer in words, all that comes out are gurgled, grunting noises. "Mmm-hem. Mmm-hem."

Dylan releases her grip and then turns, rising taller with every stride as she makes her way back to the table where Abby holds both thumbs up. "I'm impressed," she says when Dylan gets closer. "It's good to know you're so persuasive when you need to be." She leaves two fifty-dollar bills to cover the tab and tip. "Fuck this place. Let's go."

There are few details in the newspaper the next morning, and Cleve thinks little about the house fire. The rest of his day consists of short trips to Walmart, the post office, Publix, and a long lunch with a few other retirees from the department.

By five o'clock, he's in front of the TV with his book and a glass of port when an update on the house fire and missing owner catches his attention. Cleve doesn't know the name, but he recognizes something familiar about the woman. It's her eyes, and maybe the way she holds her mouth in her driver's license picture shown on the screen. Cleve closes his book and sets down his port. The woman has the exact same look in her eye as his nephew Vincent did.

The next thirty-six hours pass in a blur of partying, kissing, and Abby's unique brand of sex, not to mention her perpetual fast-talking. Dylan wakes on Sunday morning to the sound of tapping on the hotel room door. The sun beams like a spotlight through a gap in the blackout curtains, and it's enough to prove how severely the backs of her eyes hurt. Despite sleeping well, she doesn't feel rested. There's been too much partying, too much wine that Abby goaded her into drinking the night before, which fills her morning bladder with an overwhelming desire to urinate. As she throws back the sheets, a thin woman from the housekeeping staff shrieks.

"I thought you no here," she says, alarm in her eyes. "I come clean."

Not really hearing her words, Dylan uses the additional light coming in through the open door to search for Abby. She wraps the top sheet around herself and goes into the bathroom. "What the fuck?" she yells. "Is it hotel policy to wake people up like that? Don't normal people sleep in on Sundays?"

"So sorry," the woman calls. "I come back."

Dylan had expected Abby to be there when the door opened; instead, she embarrassed herself by being exposed. With Abby missing, Dylan skips her morning shower and instead just relieves herself, brushes her teeth, and dresses quickly. As she transfers her wallet, watch, and forty-three cents in loose change from a drawer into her pockets, she notices a folded piece of paper resting atop the dresser beside a modest stack of fifty-dollar bills.

The note is written on onionskin paper, like it's from the front of an old dictionary or bible. It's nearly weightless, as if it might be launched away by the cold air streaming out of the vent over her head. Two edges of the note are sharp, while the top and side of the paper is ragged, having been torn from a larger piece.

As she prepares to read the note, Dylan holds her breath and then squeezes her eyes shut with all her strength. She wants the words to say, *Be right back*, or something equally as encouraging. Instead, it says, *Get an Uber and go to the corner of 6th Avenue and 18th Street in Ybor City. Walk behind the railroad tracks and through the alley between two buildings and knock five times on the black door on the right. Long story. I'll explain later.*

P.S. I will be there. Trust me.

Dylan has never used Uber and instead calls Yellow Cab, which arrives quickly and makes good time down I-275. Sunday afternoon is the only time in the entire bay area that the roads are not crowded. On her way to Ybor City to meet up with Abby, Dylan realizes this is the first time they've been apart in the three days since the fire. With no time to waste, she's not remotely tempted to have the cab drive by her house to see what's left among the charred remains. Curiosity isn't worth losing Abby over.

Anxiety has Dylan shifting her shoulders with every click of the meter in the cab as they cross the Howard Franklin Bridge. The back of her throat is dry, and she has a hard time swallowing. What if she can't find Abby?

Ambling down 7th Avenue in Ybor City, the cab driver taps the horn as he swerves around a giant street sweeper. Dylan is surprised by how slow the thing moves in light of how many streets there are to clean.

She has a vague idea this was once the cigar capital of America, but has no idea if it still is. Her father used to smoke cigars. Dylan doesn't waste a moment contemplating it further.

The sidewalks and many of the side streets are cobbled with misshapen bricks, and the facades of the buildings are pre-depression era. Families walk up 7th Avenue toward the church. Mothers in hats, which surprises Dylan, and teenagers with their noses buried in their phone screens. The driver pulls over to a loading zone and turns off the meter that reads $47.80.

Dylan pulls out a fifty from the envelope and then rethinks a two-dollar tip. She reaches into her pocket and extracts a ten, hoping that will be enough.

"All right," the driver says, taking the money.

Law offices and banks are ubiquitous here since re-gentrification, but they're all closed on Sunday. Scattered along that end of Seventh Avenue are tourists coming in and out of antique shops, cafes, and tattoo parlors. Crews in orange vests change trash can liners filled with debris from a busy Saturday night of bar hopping along the closed-off street. All the while, Dylan cannot imagine Abby having something to do in this part of town.

To avoid the crowds, Dylan walks down 8th Avenue to 4th Street, then down the alley until she finds the red sign with a blue painted circle above a door in an alley. The black door is metal with no knob on the outside.

Dylan stands outside the building, verifies the address against numbers printed by hand. The instructions Abby wrote included no address but said to knock five times. Dylan does so, hoping this is the right door.

At first there's nothing, and then a mechanical buzzing as the door juts open automatically. Dylan enters, ducking her head. Though it's brightly lit, the place has low ceilings and she feels a little claustrophobic. A man sits behind a desk directly in front of her.

"Name?"

Dylan isn't sure she wants to respond.

"I can't let you in unless you're on the list."

Dylan looks toward a curtain along the back wall and tucks

the directions into her back pocket. "Rivers," she says. "Dylan."

The guy lays a folded Spiderman comic book on the counter and consults the clipboard on the desk. "Rivers," he says. "Yeah. Okay. You're all set. If you don't want the clothes you're wearing ripped, you can change into one of the robes you'll find on hooks along the back wall." He then hands Dylan a towel and a condom. "Use them if you want, come back if you need more."

"Excuse me?"

"It's just through the curtains. Have a good time," he says, going back to his comic book.

Dylan passes through the curtain and into a room with a couch, a hanging apparatus near the back corner, a mattress on the floor, and a low stage, where three men simultaneously have sex with one woman. Nearby, a couple dozen men stand naked playing with themselves as they wait their turn.

Spectators in various states of undress watch from the main floor. Mostly men masturbating, others who strip and join the line, but there are other women, even couples being voyeuristic or servicing each other while keeping one eye on the stage.

Dylan thinks there must be some mistake. This doesn't look like the kind of place Abby would frequent. No matter how fucked up she is, she'd never put herself through this.

Dylan drifts back, closer to the curtain and watches.

Stale cigarette smoke and the warm smell of sex fill the air. It simultaneously repulses and intrigues her. The woman at the center of the activity on stage has good features and could be pretty if not for the contortions she twists her face into. The naked men range in age from late twenties to what appears to be mid-sixties. Without clothes, it's impossible for Dylan to know if these men are doctors who work at the hospital or mechanics who change her car's oil. Haircuts and hard-ons are the only things making them different, so Dylan focuses on the woman.

After awhile the group of men changes, but the attack is the same. The woman is nude except for a black studded dog collar attached to a chain leash. Her hands are bound behind her back

141

and she's on her side. Men penetrate her in both ends, while another guy fondles her breasts. A fourth guy jangles the leash while sucking her toes and then licking her feet.

None of the people in the room speak, and aside from their intermittent grunting and the rattling of the chain leash, the only sound in the room is the barely audible moans coming from the woman until a door opens in the back of the room.

Another woman, this one dressed in what might be church clothes and sensible black shoes, frantically kicks inches above the ground as two guys in blue coveralls drag her in and pin her down onto a couch in the center of the room. Immediately, half a dozen hands tear at her clothing, all while the woman struggles and fights them.

Dylan's instinct is to run out of there, but she can't seem to make her legs move. She stands there, towel draped over her shoulder, the oily foil of a condom wrapper in her hand, and wonders what Abby has gotten her into. She's awed by the theater of it all, and she alternates her attention between the two women. The first woman looks as if her dance card has been too full for too long, but her breasts are larger than the new woman's, and they jiggle with the impact she receives. The new woman isn't as appealing, but her act of escape is compelling.

A few minutes later, another woman is led out of the door in the back of the room. This time, a woman dressed casually in shorts and a tank top, like Abby, is pulled into the room and onto the mattress in the far corner. Her act is also one of escape, as she seems to resist another group of men who tear at her clothes and push themselves into her. Dylan can't believe two similar acts would be scheduled so close together, so she focuses her attention on the new arrival, who is violently twisting and kicking, grunting with exertion. She is either the better actress or one who really doesn't want to be there.

The longer Dylan looks at the woman, the more her hair resembles Abby's. Then suddenly, the woman's body is equally as fit and her size is identical. For a moment, Dylan allows that it might actually be her. She walks the perimeter of the room to get closer and no one interferes with her progress. Once she's perpendicular to the woman, she's convinced it is Abby.

Dylan clamps off her breath and lunges forward, grabs the first pair of shoulders she can, and yanks the guy off of her.

The guy stumbles backward. "Hey, yeah. This one's feisty." He comes at her, tears at her shirt. "All right," he says, as he moves to kiss her breasts.

Another guy appears from behind. They begin pulling at her, tugging her. Forcing her body into the position of submission where they will do to her what she least wants done.

Dylan throws a forearm into the guy's head. The contact is more solid than the heavy bag at home and jars her shoulder, makes her bite her tongue. He stumbles backward. She spins and catches the guy behind her with an elbow, then swings wildly at the guy in Abby's mouth. Dylan's mind is clear, and her feet and hands are in constant motion.

She bends and lifts Abby off her back. Just then, the hair on the back of her neck raises and she hears a crash and her head grows warm in the absorption of a fist pounding into her ear. Before she can recoil or assume a defensive posture, she sees a smile creasing both sides of Abby's mouth.

Another blow rains down on Dylan. She is punched hard and often enough to drive her to the floor with her arms over her head, where bare feet kick into the ribs along her unprotected back. From this posture, she sees Abby retreat.

Two guys in coveralls jerk her up by her arms and drag her across the room, kick open the door, and toss her into the alley.

Out in the street, Dylan realizes she's still holding a condom in her closed fist. She drops it as she pushes herself up to her feet. Blood runs from her nose and her busted lip, and she wipes at the flow with the back of her wrist.

Through the darkness, she hears, "I always catch you bleeding by yourself."

Dylan stands fully upright as quickly as her bruised ribs will allow. Abby's dressed in jeans and a T-shirt, but her hair is still a mess from being groped in there. She's smiling at her. Dylan's too hurt to take a swing at her.

"Are you okay?" Abby asks.

"What the fuck was that?"

Abby takes a step toward her, swipes a finger in the blood on her face. "I had to see if you really loved me."

"By fucking guys like that?"

"It was a test," she says. "And you passed."

The next day, in their hotel room, Dylan feels like she's been run over. Hers ribs, back, and neck are all but locked, and she feels a dull ache in her jaw.

While Abby does yoga in the corner, Dylan lies prone on the bed. She has the television on but hasn't paid much attention to anything other than Abby.

"Why do you always leave on the Spanish channel? You speak Spanish?" Abby asks.

While most people watch television for entertainment, Dylan has always used television purely for the company it provided. "I guess," Dylan says.

Abby looks up from her downward dog and says, "You should put more ice on your face. Maybe that swelling and discoloration will go away in about a year."

"I'll get some later."

"I'll go get it." Abby shoots up, grabs the ice bucket, and disappears out the door. This is the nicest hotel Dylan's ever stayed in. The linens are white and crisp in their newness. None of the paint is peeling from the walls, and she doesn't hear yelling in the hall when Abby returns with the ice.

She hands Dylan a washcloth, ties a knot in the ice bucket liner, then rests the cold bag on her face.

As the ice settles onto the contours of her swollen face, Abby tugs down her underwear. "Maybe this will make you feel better," she says, hot breath wafting across Dylan's exposed scars and new wound, which Abby is about to continue.

Abby lifts her mouth, bends her elbow, and holds the razor in the other hand by her ear as if it were a pen and she was pausing to ponder a clue in a crossword puzzle. "I know I've been asking a lot of you, but roll with it. Okay? We're close to having something really special."

Once Abby puts her mouth back on Dylan again, Dylan lays her head back. This is by far the most special period of her life. She won't tell Abby that though, because she doesn't want to talk—not now, not ever. She just wants to absorb everything about this woman and spend every fucking minute with her and she will do whatever that requires.

Afterward, Abby comes out of the bathroom with a bottle of nail polish. "Flip around the dial while I do this. Maybe when I'm done, we'll go pick up some weed."

When Abby sits on the side chair and tucks her legs to do her toes, Dylan says, "I'll do that."

"Really?"

Dylan takes the brush and bottle from her and kneels down. The last time she painted another woman's toenails happened on New Year's Eve, just months before her fourteenth birthday: Dylan and Mom sat on the couch together in a base house surrounded by hundreds of similar concrete structures in the foothills of Subic Bay, watching a Christmas parade complicated by snow on their old black and white dial set. Television programming came delayed a minimum of one week on the Armed Forces Radio & Television Service, having to travel the distance to the middle of the Pacific Ocean. But they sat there, watching the floats, bands, and crowds line the streets of some big city while firecrackers popped outside their window. Darkness had yet to set in. Her father, already gone for the first month of his six-month deployment, made the holidays better by his absence. Gone. At sea. Underway. The terms varied, but the joy felt the same. At this point of his absence, Mom began coming out of her emotional hibernation. Since Christmas passed, she went to the commissary once, and she even made dresses in brighter colors and out of fancier fabric.

Out of the blue, Mom said, "I bought a bottle of nail polish at the Exchange the other day and I think it is high time I polished my nails."

When Mom got up, Dylan assumed she'd come right back, but she didn't. It wasn't like her to be gone for so long. When they were alone in the house, she usually had Dylan right beside her. With the fireworks going off well before midnight, she'd been surprised she left her side at all.

Outside, kids had fireworks shooting in all sizes and directions. The *pops* and *booms* unnerved Dylan enough to get off the couch and find Mom. The noise might have caused her to lock herself in the bathroom again.

But when Dylan went to find her, she wasn't in the bathroom, but rather in her room and calm. Mom sat precariously on the edge of the bed, one bare leg extended, the other bent up, heel on the mattress. Her housecoat rode up her thighs and Dylan saw the white panel of her panties.

"What are you doing?"

"What does it look like?"

Dylan knew the intent of the action, but she'd never actually seen her do it.

"This is none too comfortable, I can tell you that," Mom said. "I'm not as limber as I used to be."

Dylan ran through the doorway and slid, the waistband of her tight corduroy pants digging into her as carpet burned her knees through the material. "I'll do it for you."

"No, no."

"It'll be easy," Dylan said. "I'm right here."

"How steady are your hands?"

Dylan raised her arms and offered up the backs of her hands to show motionless fingers.

"Okay, but just the nails. Don't get any paint on the toes. I'll never be able to get it off."

Dylan took the bottle from her with one hand and the brush in the other. The fumes of the polish and the *pops* and *booms* outside were intoxicating. She found something so violent and yet so soothing there at her mother's feet. Her eyes level with her mother's hips, Dylan couldn't make herself look away from the area between the back of her thigh and buttock subdivided by the scalloped elastic trim of her panties. Dylan dipped the brush into the bottle and prepared to paint the toes on the raised foot, but Mom extended her bent leg, crossing one foot over the other. Suddenly, Dylan felt self-conscious for being so high up from the area to be painted. "Oh," she said.

"What? Is that no good?"

"No," Dylan said, sitting back on her heels. "It's fine."

On the way down to her feet, she took in the length of her mother's bare legs, saw the dark stubble of unshaven hair set against the blue-green tint of varicose veins that fascinated her. At her feet, Dylan uncrossed her mother's ankles and set her left foot against her thigh to give her a better angle on the nails. This also gave Dylan another glimpse at the white shock of panties at her crotch, but she focused her attention on her mother's feet.

Dylan worked baby toe to big toe, employing subtle, even strokes as if touching up a masterpiece. After every toe, she stuck the brush back into the bottle and followed her mother's legs with her eyes, checking to see if that white cotton panel was still visible, and blew on each toe. As she finished the left big toe, she could have sworn she saw Mom throw her head back and sigh, but she was a child and uncertain of sighs. So she focused again on the crotch only inches from her face before bending down to again blow on the areas she'd just painted.

As Mom lifted her foot off Dylan's thigh, Dylan noticed her own crotch. Her corduroys were suddenly wet there and she felt a strange sensation, but was too embarrassed and unsure about it to mention it. Instead, Dylan replaced the left foot with the right and leaned in to paint the baby toe.

"You're doing excellent work," Mom said, looking down, her palms on the bed.

Dylan said nothing, but continued painting, hoping to finish so she could go to the bathroom before pee came out.

Cleve calls the Eidolon Corporation on Monday morning to find out more about this Dylan Rivers. Using the excuse of wishing to express his condolences to the young woman's boss, Cleve figures he will get some information without officially interfering. The woman on the phone launches into the story and is still talking when Cleve hangs up.

Dylan sits in the passenger seat while Abby drives into eastern Hillsborough County, exiting the interstate at the second Brandon exit. Dylan feels straightjacketed by the pressure not to drive. "A fender bender or a speed trap could put all our fun on hold. It's not worth it. There will be time to drive later," Abby says.

Dylan's only experience with this part of the county came from reading the Heritage section of the *Tribune* on Sundays. Brandon once stood proudly as cattle country. Now, strip plazas and big-box stores crowd the horizon to the point she can barely envision green space enough for cows to graze. There are dozens of apartment complexes right along the main road and traffic is heavy at every intersection.

Abby hugs the wheel as she pulls into one of the many subdivisions. She bites her lip and says, "He's at 1684."

"This is still the 1800 block," Dylan says. As she leans forward to concentrate on the passing numbers, the sound of lawn care crews with their mowers, edgers, and blowers fills the air, yet she doesn't actually see anyone, only their trucks and trailers. She's always envied those who work outdoors.

Abby nods. "There it is. One-six-eight-four."

Dylan's never been to a drug deal before, but she has to accompany Abby. Beyond any semblance of protecting her, she doesn't want to give Abby the opportunity to disappear.

Approaching the door, loud Tejano music escapes, making Dylan uncomfortable. The idea of the neighbors associating her with a party on a Monday afternoon makes her hold her breath. Abby rings the bell and then uses a thumbnail to flick the backs of the other nails. Dylan continues to hold her breath. No matter how annoying that tick-ticking sound gets, she'll never complain.

After waiting maybe a minute for someone to answer the doorbell, Abby pounds on his door. "We don't have all day," she says, then checks her watch. It's a man's watch with a big dial and a leather strap. It's the one thing Dylan doesn't find attractive on or in her. Over the past four days she's learned to accept it.

A chain on the other side slides and the door cracks open. "You Lawton's people?"

Dylan can't see anyone there, but Abby says, "Awesome Sanchez! You know me. I'm Abby. Lawton's sister."

"Huh? Oh. Yeah. Right. Lawton's fine-ass sister." Awesome Sanchez swings the door open. He's got bushy red hair and is barrel-chested, and Dylan instantly recognizes him as the shirtless guy in the brown bandana from the party at Abby's house.

His bare torso and arms, nearly translucent as they are, are relatively covered in tattoos. He's decidedly intimidating, but obviously Irish. He then parts his lips to reveal the scalloped edge of his rounded teeth. Under different circumstances, his expression might not pass for a smile. "Yeah. Come on in," he says. Behind him a Japanese flag is tacked to the wall with a deer head mounted in the center.

Once inside, he looks over to Dylan. "Whoa, dude. Are you a chick MMA fighter?"

Dylan looks to Abby. "What's that?"

"No," Abby says. "She got into a small riot with a bunch of douche bags in Ybor last night."

"Huh?" he says. "Oh, right. Ybor."

Dylan wants to respond, but there's no way to explain it better than Abby's summary—riot. Besides, she doesn't really care what this guy thinks of her. Abby is another matter. Her black eye no longer shows through her makeup, but Dylan isn't sure if this Awesome Sanchez guy thinks the faint discoloration is anything more than a lack of sleep. Nothing Awesome Sanchez says implies that he sees anything other than the marks on her own face. He fondles his phone as he stares at Abby.

Dylan is uncomfortable in the following silence, but instead of holding her breath, she interjects, "Excuse me, but is that water I hear running?"

Awesome Sanchez doesn't take his eyes off Abby. "Huh? Oh yeah. Probably. We have to keep a hose in the tank. You know. Evaporation, she's a bitch."

"Evaporation?"

"Huh? Oh, the hydro."

"The hydro?"

Abby cuts in. "He grows water-based plants."

"Hey, hold up," he says. "It ain't plants I grow."

"No, then what do you call it?"

"Huh? I grow love, baby. A special strain of chronic I call J-Rain. Shit's so sweet you think you was smoking candy. I'll hook you up."

"What will that cost me?"

"Huh? Oh. In cash? Four hundred dollars. In time? About twenty minutes on the other side of that door over there."

"We've got the cash, thanks," Dylan says, fanning out the wad of fifties left over from Abby's note the day before.

"Huh?" Awesome Sanchez says for the thousandth time. "Oh, it seems your mother doesn't want you going away with me."

"She's not my mother. You know that."

"Huh? Oh, that's okay. You know what, I'm going to make a new strain of chronic. I'll cross pollinate some Puchong tealeaves and call it Battered Princess. You like that, baby?"

Dylan's fists clench, but she doesn't act. If Abby doesn't care enough to assert herself, then fuck it.

"I just want the weed and some pills," Abby says.

"What's your pleasure?"

"TDX."

"TDX? You looking to party?"

"Private party. I need a hundred."

"Huh? I don't deal opioids in that quantity."

"Can't handle the order?"

"Huh? I don't want nobody selling without setting up a franchise fee."

"I'm not going to sell. It's for personal consumption."

In the space of that pause, Dylan hears a dog bark. The sound of each bark reminds her of smacks with a wet belt across her back and neck. Dylan never had a dog.

"A hundred pills?" Awesome Sanchez says. "You going Ted Lee Dorn or something? You plan on taking churchgoers to a better place like he did or something? What do you need with so many pills?"

"I told you. Personal consumption."

"Huh? Then why buy a six-month supply?"

"I'm not too fond of the drive out here."

"I'll deliver smaller quantities to your place. To your bedroom. You know?"

"Next time I might just take you up on that, but for now, I'd rather take them with me. You know?"

"Huh? But it will be so long until I see you again."

"I mean, I'm splitting them with her," she says, pointing to Dylan. "And she's got a high tolerance. So it will be much sooner than you think."

Awesome Sanchez bends down and rubs Abby's bare leg up to the hem of her shorts. Instead of cupping her ass, he tucks his fingers into the subtle apex of leg and ass cheek, his hand gripping her thigh for a moment then stands up, licks his lips, and squints at her. "That many pills will cost you twenty-five hundred dollars, unless you want to take it out in trade right here, right now."

Abby removes an envelope from her purse. "There's three thousand dollars in here. Throw in a few extras, and then a few more."

Dylan feels perspiration bead on her forehead, and she casually wipes at the wetness with the back of her hand. She doesn't know if it's nerves or if it is really that hot in the house. As she dries her hand on her pants leg, Awesome Sanchez says, "Sorry about the heat. I've got grow lamps in the other room. Puts out a shitload of heat. Piece of shit air conditioner can't keep up."

"It's fine," Dylan lies. "I'm cool.'

With the exception of checking his phone, Awesome Sanchez doesn't stop smiling at Abby. Though it annoys her, Dylan understands.

Abby doesn't let it go. She says, "It's cooler outside. Why don't you open the windows?"

"Huh?" Awesome Sanchez says, looking at her. "Oh, I don't want no one knowing my business. You know? Can't trust nobody. No problems. I've got a five-ton Puron unit coming next week. You know, before the summer hits."

As Awesome Sanchez begins counting out the pills, his phone rings. He answers in Spanish. Dylan listens as Awesome Sanchez speaks the Cuban dialect. It sounds ridiculous coming out of his freckled face. It's fast and Dylan can't get every word, but she understands enough to know that Awesome Sanchez is telling his buddy on the other end how he could beat the rest of the shit out of the other bitch and bang this fine-ass woman. He goes on about Abby's shit-chute. Dylan holds her breath for the remainder of the conversation. The blood pounding in her ears is almost loud enough to block out Awesome Sanchez's conversation, but not completely. Abby is looking back and forth between them. She apparently has no idea what that pig is saying about her.

* * *

Though the phone call seems to distract Awesome Sanchez for a moment, his eyes never leave Abby. She's used to stares and the leering, and this guy has seen her naked up on stage at Rifley's, so she imagines he's picturing her naked now. It doesn't bother her to any great degree. Let this pale fucker have the visions in his head. It's as close as he will ever get. She's used to dancing on stage or behind the voyeuristic pane of glass as men in booths feed dollar bills to keep the windows open. It's the same thing. The bulging stares, straining to open even wider. Every man looks somewhere in particular. Some are breast men, some are ass men. Others want nothing but to see the fleshy folds of hairless genitalia. So few look at her face. Almost no one ever makes eye contact.

Even on the street. Random men try to see through her clothes so often that performing is easy. At least being on stage pays. Being down amongst them is like giving previews for free. Free views. That's the game, and she plays it with Awesome Sanchez in the hopes of getting more than she'll pay for. He looks more like a school kid infatuated with a new teacher than a port authority official moonlighting as a drug dealer, growing the best weed in the entire state. He's rattling off a bunch of sentences in Spanish, and she doesn't understand a single word.

When he hangs up, Dylan springs into the air, flies over the couch and lands an elbow into Awesome Sanchez's head. The guy absorbs the blow with quiet agony and tips sideways onto the couch, spilling the better part of an ounce of his primo weed onto his lap. There's a mad clanging of candleholders and paraphernalia as the two wrestle themselves off the couch. Violence as swift as this, especially when combined with the ass-beating Dylan took in Ybor, is beyond romantic. Each blow that she rains down on Awesome Sanchez is like a love letter. Each smack of her fist is like a rose petal and part of Abby never wants it to end. "Okay," she finally says. "That's enough."

With his thumb, Awesome Sanchez locates the deepest contusion on Dylan's forehead and pushes it like a melon. Dylan grunts in agony, but it sounds like a weightlifter's exhale and it somehow gives her the power to grab Awesome Sanchez's legs out from under him. With her free hand, Dylan knocks loose the grip on her head and then pounds him in the face repeatedly. Vibrations like bass drum kicks throb through Abby with each whack. Dylan hollers in Spanish, and though Abby can't make out the words, she's sure they're expletives.

Dylan pushes herself up to her knees and rains blows onto the guy's head and face until her hands grow tired.

But instead of stopping, she rises from the couch and grabs the scale from the coffee table and swats down with it, repeatedly, as if she were chopping firewood.

Abby jumps onto Dylan. "That's enough," she says wrapping her arms and legs around her in the process. "You're going to decapitate him." She then kisses Dylan deeply and fully. Dylan fights her mouth away from Abby's, which gives her the time to say, "That was fucking amazing. You totally kicked that mother-fucker's ass."

Dylan's eyes gloss up at Abby a little wider than normal, then narrow as her face creases into a smile. "What now?"

"Awesome Sanchez has friends, family, and customers who will miss him. Such behavior will make you even more of a target with the authorities." With this in mind, Abby resolves to shield Dylan with all her strength, because if she gets caught now, her time with her will be wasted and she will be on the other side.

Awesome Sanchez lays crumpled and bleeding on the wood floor.

"I think I killed him," Dylan says, sucking on the first knuckle on her right hand. "We better get out of here."

"Are you kidding?"

Dylan grabs her by the arm, which, ordinarily, Abby would have liked, but now it's in panic, not passion.

"Fuck that," Abby says, and pulls her arm free. "We came for something I'd rather not leave without."

"Are you kidding?"

"How much do you think we should take?"

Dylan looks in the direction of a very prone Awesome Sanchez and then shrugs. "It's not like he's going to be in the mood to take inventory anytime soon."

"Yeah. Fuck him," Abby says. "He could have hurt you."

"What about you? Are you all right?"

"I'm fine. I'm fine. But don't you think we should check on him?"

Dylan doesn't speak. She continues to breathe into her fist for a few minutes, then says, "Maybe we should call 9-1-1."

Abby looks up from stuffing the bag of pills and a few handfuls of the mountainous pot from the coffee table into her purse. "I was kidding. Shit. Don't be so gullible. Hand me that pillowcase draped over the headrest, would you?"

As she hands it over, Dylan says, "I couldn't let him get away with that shit he was talking about you."

"No. No. It's cool," Abby says hugging her. "You smell like franks and pennies." Abby's not certain it's pennies, but there's a scent of dirty change and pork products. It's a common feral element she's found only in certain people along the way, men mostly, and she's glad Dylan has it. This is when she smells sexiest to her. "I fucking love it," Abby says. "Come on. Let's get out of here."

Cleve drives by Rifley's in the afternoon, hoping it will be less busy and eventful than the last time he'd been there. The guy at the door wears a sleeveless T-shirt to show off tattoos around his shoulders and neck. His lip is pierced badly in the center of a full goatee. It's hard to look away from the raw wound there.

"Afternoon," Cleve says.

"Welcome back."

"You recognize me?" Cleve points to his own chest.

"Have you been here before?"

"Well, yes. Once, actually."

"Well then, welcome back."

Cleve flashes his badge at the guy. "Ah, man. We're done to death with talking about that guy that croaked in here last week. What more is there to say, man?"

"It's not about that. Now look, I need to speak with Rifley."

"He's out today. Sailing in the Bahamas."

"When will he be back?"

"Can't say."

"Well, can you tell me if Cassandra is working today?"

"Ain't seen her in about a week. That ain't unusual though. She comes in when she wants."

"Thank you for your help," Cleve says. "Take care of that lip."

They spend Wednesday inside the hotel room, glued to Bay News 9 and CNN to see if there are any reports about the incident with Awesome Sanchez or any follow-ups on Dylan's house. They'd each taken a TDX, just to smooth the edges, and Abby knows Dylan's totally lifted when she says she's ready to go out.

Abby isn't convinced that it's safe to leave the hotel room. What worries her isn't the cops—Dylan is virtually unrecognizable from her driver's license picture now that she's restyled her hair and has contusions on her face, but she's not sure Awesome Sanchez doesn't have some friends or business associates after her. Abby leaves the room, promising to bring Dylan a new bag of ice for her sore spots, but her real mission leads her to the gift shop to buy a pair of scissors.

Returning to the room, she says, "Have you ever cut hair before, Dylan?"

"Just my own."

"Well then, I might as well do it myself."

"You're cutting your hair?"

"Is that a big deal for you?"

"No, but—"

"If Awesome Sanchez is still alive or if any of his crew knows I was at his house, they might come looking for me. A lot of people around here know me."

"How short?"

"Just short enough to make me look completely different to men."

While Dylan cuts her hair, Abby checks out of the room electronically via the television, and after dropping their bags in the car, they walk.

The night air and cool moisture off the bay surprises Abby's newly bare neck and sends a shiver through her. There are so few nights where temperatures are perfect, and if the clumps of hair she cut were on her head instead of circulating in the bay-area sewage system, she'd be fine. Aside from the hair, this is one of those nights she's happy to be out amongst people. While she walks with an air of importance in her platform espadrilles, Dylan sulks along, the black eyes and red welts splayed across her face a stark contrast to her white shirt and dirty khaki pants.

She's beaten down and she looks as if she's all but ready for what Abby has in mind.

Abby adjusts her purse so the strap bisects her breasts beneath her clingy blue top. With her hands free, she reaches for Dylan's hand and interlaces her fingers with hers as they walk.

A man in linen shorts and a flowing, untucked shirt with TOMMY BAHAMA emblazoned across the back lights a cigar from one of the tiki torches lining the path. Dylan watches a woman in a sundress stride up to hook her arm through his and they continue on their way past Abby and Dylan. "I don't belong here," Dylan says.

"Where?"

"Anywhere, really." Dylan isn't there as she speaks. "My origins aren't rooted thanks to the military. I've never felt like I belonged. I'm a perpetual tourist."

Abby doesn't respond other than to firm her grip on Dylan's hand with her fingers.

They keep walking, but their pace is slow enough to hear the cars passing on I-275 in the distance. Dylan looks away, and says, "I'm arid. I'm a fucking arctic desert." She then wraps her arm around Abby's shoulders. "I never worried about it because it allowed me to get wrapped up in work. Completely. A little too completely, obviously."

Abby shifts her position to follow along. Just then a pair of joggers rounds the corner and Dylan nods to say hello when they pass. Abby says, "I'm a year older than Lawton is, you know?"

Dylan looks at her without expression.

"I was held back in case there were to be no male heirs and my father thought being a female would necessitate 'all possible advantages to level the playing field.'"

"Lots of kids are held back a grade."

"No," Abby says, then stops. She wonders if Dylan is even listening to a word she says. "We were raised as twins. Okay? He doesn't know."

"That's fucked up."

Abby takes this opportunity to change the subject. "How are you feeling right now?"

"I'm feeling that pill, all slowed down and rubbery. But I'm still worried in all the usual ways, I suppose."

"Haven't you always been?" Abby says, picking needles off the waist-high evergreen near the path.

"What do you think will happen?" Dylan's voice is soft and childlike.

"What do you mean?" Abby asks, though she knows exactly what Dylan's getting at.

"My name is attached to that house. I'm sure there are tons of legal affairs and all sorts of paperwork to get in order."

Abby wishes she could yank down Dylan's pants and take the blade to her skin right then in an effort to distract her. "Fuck them."

"Don't you think they'll find me...eventually?"

* * *

Dylan walks half a pace behind Abby, watching her walk as she pulls a wadded piece of paper from her back pocket. She pauses by a trash can and unfolds the paper only to wad it up again and toss it into the receptacle. "Tell me about your mother," Abby says.

Dylan thinks of the sewing form, crushed and saturated in her driveway. Her former driveway. She resumes walking with her. "She sort of divorced reality." The words come out of her casually. She lets her head float on her neck as she speaks. "It's not like she was straightjacketed in a padded room. It wasn't like that." Then she stops talking. One hand goes to cover her mouth as she coughs, wondering if the beach air is getting to her. "Long as I can remember, she hid in the house. Too scared to leave. Blonde hair in a bun, brown eyes like empty circles— knocked-out holes, like a field rabbit hiding in tall grass. She grew to be that useless."

A shut in. She didn't leave the house for anything. Dylan shopped for groceries every week from the time she turned ten. People at the commissary knew her by name. "Mom passed time watching videos from the collection of tapes she kept in a footlocker by the sagging sofa. Her favorite was *The Wizard of Oz.*"

One day, she asked Dylan to sit amongst her pile of wadded-up tissues and watch it with her. Dylan would have volunteered, just to be close to her. Sharing time like that, not talking, not interacting at all, just staring at images of people on the screen. As if that could provide any sense of closeness. "Mom said, 'I wish I were Dorothy. I'd like to get blown away to another time and place.'"

The statement didn't hurt. In a way, Dylan understood. Related. Dylan handed her a fresh tissue and she flinched at the tiny cloud of tissue dust. "Every time she heard a noise, Mom made Dorothy's lion look like a gladiator by comparison. Phone ringing, she flinched and bit her lip. Church bells in the distance, she hid in her hands. Planes taking off, she wrapped a pillow over her head. My father's voice? She locked herself in the bathroom. For hours."

Dylan wanted to help, reach out, in some way. To touch her heart, comfort her soul. To tell her everything would be okay, that she could get through it. Because she loved her mom. And hated her father. Dylan no longer felt fear, but she understood how Mom could. Her skin didn't bounce back from punches as quickly as hers. Mom's face stayed dented longer, like damaged aluminum cans at the commissary. Her eyes held the raccoon circles longer than Dylan's.

"She'd stopped functioning outside of the house or her housecoat years prior. She cried harder every day. Some days that was all she did, even while watching *The Wizard of Oz* together."

Dylan tried to do everything she no longer did. She tried to make the house look perfect. She learned to cook the foods her father demanded. To keep peace. To buy time.

Dylan's recollections of the final days with her are impossible to nail down. "One night, Mom found her yellow brick road. Just like Dorothy. Unfortunately, that shining path proved a lonely stretch of highway. The only freeway near the base."

From what Dylan pieced together from the police and her father, Mom hit the road, barefoot, to escape God knows what—her father, her, herself. But still, she can't picture any of it. Can't remember if she ever said goodbye.

"Wow," Abby says, pulling Dylan's head into her shoulder.

Abby recognizes this as the perfect time, but she's almost too nervous to say what it's time to say. She's only been far enough to have this conversation with one other person, a guy, and he said no and never returned her calls. In her opinion, though, Dylan is a far stronger candidate than that nutbag Vincent.

She continues plucking at foliage as they walk around the park. "Endings," she finally says tugging on pine needles from an evergreen. "Endings define the random shit that happens before. You know? I want my death to give my life shape. On my terms. You know? I can be at my peak forever."

"What the fuck does that even mean?"

"I'm talking about the getting old part. I don't want any fucking part of that."

"Well, sixty these days is a lot different than it was in previous generations. More active and all. By the time you get there, gray hair will be a goal."

"You just go ahead and believe that," Abby says. "What do you want people to say about you when you're dead?"

"I've never given it any thought."

Abby spots a homeless man on a bench at the corner of the courtyard surrounded by hibiscus and evergreen bushes. She's well within view to notice one shoe is off, and a grotesque sock is tucked up around his toes as he picks some sort of scabs off his feet. She's repulsed, but she can't help looking in that general direction. His other shoe is a red Chuck Taylor high-top with holes fraying in the canvas. His face might lead you to believe his parents were an old, bitter Slavic woman and a beagle. The guy isn't old, but old-ish. The best Abby can guess is the nebulous age bracket somewhere between thirty and seventy, and even from this distance, he appears to have all the traits of someone who smells. He's just gross. Picking and scratching and setting up camp with his shopping cart partially wedged between the hibiscus and evergreen foliage behind his bench.

"Life is about quality, not quantity," Abby says. "Besides, do you want to go back and pay your debt to society and then get another mind-numbing job just so you can pay the bills for twenty or thirty more years of the same shit? Do you really want to grow old? Or are you just so bent on aging and growing frail that you'll yoke yourself back up and keep towing the feces cart? More tedium, more discontent." She's rehearsed this speech a dozen times in the mirror.

"Why do you hate life so much?"

Abby hates the bum. Instinctively. Everyone she knows has softer feelings for the homeless. Their hearts bleed at the thought of someone not having at least the basic necessities of modern convenience. "You've got it backwards. I fucking love life. I just want to end it before...See that old man there?" she says, pointing to a guy walking from a rental car toward the pier.

"Yeah."

"He's bald. He's overweight, and if tradition holds true, he has to get up three to five times a night to piss and he hasn't had sex in at least three years. If he were a leased car, he should have turned himself in long ago, because now his paint is faded, his interior is trashed and parts are starting to fall off of him."

"He seems to be enjoying his high-mileage."

"Maybe, but it doesn't compare to the new car smell. And it isn't worth anything. He's way past the value of his residual."

"You make it sound so zero-sum. What is this? Some sort of extreme-sport Buddhism or something? Jesus Christ."

"No. Not at all. Buddhists believe in shunning all desire. I say overdose on desire before you drown in the inevitable."

Dylan stops, looks behind her, and back to Abby. "What the fuck does that mean?"

"It's simple." Abby stands facing Dylan. Switches hands and places one on her shoulder. "Aging doesn't interest me. My mother has had eleven elective surgeries and two of the mandatory kinds. I won't do that, and I don't like the projected picture. Worse still, no matter what I do or don't do, there's nothing that could ever fix the cumulative effects the living world will face. Don't you see? Aging, Dylan...the human body is perpetually in a state of decay. We're rotting. All of us. As we stand here, right this instant, enzymes and bacteria are breaking down organs and our bones are growing even more brittle. Old age. Jesus. The gel in our eyes and between our joints is drying up and we're starting to shrink and creak. Don't tell me you haven't noticed."

"My back gets sore, sure."

Abby cups Dylan's face in her hands. "That's only going to get worse. Then it'll be other things. Hospitalizations, spending all your money to keep from being uncomfortable. Time is the enemy. Why wait around for dentures and bypasses? Haven't you ever thought about how much more exciting it would be to beat time? To say the ultimate 'fuck you' to the cycle of life?"

When the soft breeze changes directions, Abby hears a wordless version of an old Elton John song playing on speakers she can't see. She's surprised the city invested the money to have the place wired for sound. It's either that or some condo dweller is feeling frisky and cranking up their surround sound system. Either way, she hates the song. Hates the saccharine nature of the whole fucking genre.

"I really don't know what to say here," Dylan says.

Abby expects Dylan to dismiss her as being too young or too idealistic. Most of the introverted people she's tried to pair up with were guilty of this. "Don't be freaked out," she says.

One guy she hooked up with in Fresno overcompensated for an extremely small penis by exercising nonstop and thrill seeking. He planned to bike the distance to the Golden Gate Bridge and then BASE jump with her, but when she recommended they should do it without parachutes, he told her he found her karma too dark suddenly, and they went their separate ways. Abby had been up for neither the bike ride nor the jump. She now wants to avoid anything too easy or cliché as jumping or shooting or a car crash. She wants something unusual. Something memorable.

"If I was completely opposed to the idea," Dylan says, "I wouldn't be with you this far. Believe me. I mean, I've always entertained the thought. Don't you think that every time I make one of these scars I want to tear the blade up my veins? I could have cut into an artery in my neck or leg and been done with it dozens of times, but I didn't. To this day I don't know why. But now, everything seems possible."

"Why don't we do it together?"

"Together?"

"Don't you want to be with me?"

"It's just a wild thing to think about."

"Chalk it up to ne plus ultra," Abby says. "The pinnacle."

"But you're so young."

"Hey, look," Abby says. "There's no pressure. I mean, I can find somebody else. A real Romeo." The second she says it, she regrets it. Not just because it's a lie, but because it has to be Dylan. There is no time to find anyone else. She doesn't want anybody else. "If you don't do it, I'll never cut you again. If you do do it, we'll be forever linked in the afterlife where I can do anything and everything to you every day and all night, every night."

Words like "all" and "every" tend to stimulate some people's sense of scope, subliminally or otherwise, and she is confident Dylan will do anything to be near her.

"The Japanese call it *Shinju*," Abby says. "The oneness of two hearts. We will be proving our love and ensuring a never-ending union."

"Will we have adjoining graves?"

"Sure thing. We'll write a detailed note before we do it. Okay?"

Dylan paces around like a yard dog; her head down, her focus narrowed to the spot in front of her. "Yeah," she says, looking up at Abby. "You know what? Fuck yeah."

Abby feels a sensation, deep in her pelvis, like a zipper being lifted up to her throat from the inside. She should have stopped talking sooner. Her birthday is tomorrow and she doesn't plan to see it or any other after it, but now her breath crowds her throat and she can't get any air. Her skin gets clammy. It's all out there and Dylan's in. She leans an arm out toward a light pole to give her counterbalance and lands on the wooden bench along the walkway, weak with the knowledge that it will finally happen.

* * *

Dylan watches Abby cross her legs, as if adding punctuation to her last statement. She feels alive, knowing she's going to die.

Before she can say anything further, Abby says, "I was pregnant once," and sighs. "It's funny. I got pregnant while my parents told me to abstain. They wanted me to abort, save family face. I was only seventeen. I got drunk when I found out. Gin, of all things. It's the last time I ever drank the stuff. Ended up crashing my car in a stupor. Head on into a telephone pole. It was a BMW convertible. Only a year old. My sweet sixteen present. Lost my baby in the crash. Doctors told me my body fat was too low to sustain the baby and I would have eventually miscarried anyway."

When Abby cries, her eyes lock onto that dead space of middle distance. The skin on her nose and cheeks glows red beneath the tears. Her inhales grow labored and little strings of spit form at the corners of her mouth, and all Dylan wants to do is bundle her up, protect her, and carry her home. Abby looks at Dylan. "I'm sorry."

"No need to apologize."

"No. It's not cool. I shouldn't cry. Everything is my choice. Right?"

Dylan has no idea what she means, but she says, "Sure." Getting caught in the lie couldn't possibly make her look worse than ignorance could.

Abby's cell phone rings, an uncharacteristically classical song that Dylan recognizes but can't name because she's never taken the time to learn the difference between Mozart and Beethoven. Abby extracts her silver-backed all-in-one and looks at the screen.

"It's Star," she says. "Fucking wonderful."

It rings twice more with the same elegant clip. Dylan still can't place the title. "You want me to...you know?"

Instead of answering, Abby catapults the phone right onto the cement beneath her. The impact is a quick burst of plastic and glass grating on concrete. It's the most uncomfortable Dylan's felt around Abby and she wants to put an end to it. Through habit, she reverts to her rigid self, the one that relies on business speak to get her through awkward conversations. But she holds her breath, realizing she's got to be a better version of herself around Abby.

"Motherfucker!" Abby shouts.

"I'm sorry," Dylan says.

"Not you. Star. That motherfucker. I'm not going to give her the satisfaction. It's too late. I hope she regrets being a bitch to me for the rest of her life."

"Wow. She must have fucked something up severely."

"Not really. But I don't care. I'm not going to spend any part of my time on Earth listening to someone try to rationalize why they did something remotely fucked up that they shouldn't have done in the first place."

She looks over her knees at the smashed phone on the ground. "Shit. I probably should call Lawton."

Dylan shrugs.

"So..." Abby says.

"So what?"

"Are you going to make me ask?"

"Ask what?"

"Why are you being such an asshole right now? Just let me use your goddamn phone."

"What phone?"

"Your fucking cell phone."

The notion strikes Dylan as absurd, in the way clean jokes are absurd, and she laughs. "I don't have a cell phone."

"How could you not have a cell phone?"

"What would I need with a cell phone?"

"I don't know. Maybe communications with the outside world like the rest of us."

"That's what email is for. And, as of recently, I've been talking to you quite a bit, in person."

"You're an odd fucking duck sometimes, Dylan Rivers."

Dylan recognizes sarcasm in the slight creases of her eyes and the way her lips meet just off center. By this point, she's no longer amazed that she notices Abby's facial features; she's come to anticipate them. Each expression on her face is a visual payoff for something that stimulates her, and Dylan no longer makes pretenses to disguise her stares.

Thirty minutes later, Dylan still walks aimlessly through the park with Abby. The downtown buildings along 4th Avenue are now behind them along with all reminders of her corporate life. Her former life. The cobblestones surrounding the fountain are engraved with the names of people who donated fifty dollars or more to keep the old Florida feel with a tin-roofed gazebo at the other end of the park. The seashell fountain trickles a slow water-fall from one plateau to another. "I've always loved the sound of rushing water," Abby says. "It makes me remember waves sloshing against the seawall along Bayshore."

They keep walking, but Abby stutter steps as she extracts something from her purse wrapped in newspaper and hands it to Dylan. It's a weighty rectangular package.

"What's this?"

"Something I want you to have," Abby says, running her fingertips upward on her exposed triceps. "Go on, open it."

Beneath the *Tampa Bay Times* wrapping is a knife with a gold bear embossed in the handle. Even folded, Dylan guesses the blade to be four inches long. "What's this?"

"This was my grandmother's," Abby says. "Used to keep it in her purse, just in case. I want you to have it."

"Really?" Dylan asks, her voice perking up a scale higher than she feels comfortable with. She clears her throat and tries again. "I mean, what for?"

"Just in case." Abby winks when she says it and takes the newsprint from Dylan and tosses it a foot from the trash can.

Dylan walks around Abby and doubles back to retrieve the newspaper.

"Don't worry about that," Abby says.

"I can't just leave it."

"It'll be fine."

Dylan stands, her right hand holding the knife. "Well, what am I supposed to do with this?"

"Put it in your pocket. It is a pocketknife, after all. You never know when it might come in handy."

It's strange to receive a gift. No one had gotten her a gift in her recent memory. But giving her something like a knife is like giving an alcoholic a bottle of booze. She can only hope Abby will use the knife on her later the night.

As they complete a lap of the park, Abby spots another homeless man, this one lying on a bench in the far corner. She wants to walk closer to the man, but Dylan hops up on the low cement retaining wall bordering a hibiscus hedge. As she entwines their fingers, she's snapped back like a dog at the end of its chain. Standing there between Dylan's spread legs, she looks at the blankness in her eyes. She feels guilty for using Dylan this way, but it has to be her. Still though, she wishes she could see how this might play out.

She remains standing, but rests against Dylan, placing her head in her chest as her body weighs down on her legs and lap and breathes in the smell of franks and pennies. The TDX pills are kicking in full blast and Abby is flat-out high. She took an extra pill in the hotel earlier while Dylan used the bathroom, but even with just one Dylan has to be fucked up now. Fucked up enough for one more test. "You see that homeless man on the bench over there?"

"Yeah."

"What do you think his deal is?"

"What do you mean? You're interested in him?"

"Relax. I'd rather fuck a doorknob or an animal than that guy. I mean, why is he homeless? You know? I mean, do you think he's happy like that?"

Dylan shrugs and says, "He looks comfortable enough. Getting by."

Abby caresses the bandage she put on Dylan's thigh earlier. She has to know the rewards waiting if she does this for her, if she passes this final test. "He needs someone to put him out of his misery," she says, then describes what she wants Dylan to do.

Dylan's breathing grows from the ache in her ribs. Her face feels like it's been through a meat grinder, but she wouldn't trade places with this homeless guy for anything. She laughs at the irony, but her cheekbones hurt too bad to sustain any kind of levity. She's closer to this homeless guy than she ever thought she'd be. Her khaki pants are as dirty as the olive-green fatigues the homeless man is wearing, but at least she's been sleeping in a hotel room instead of on a bench. In the distance, the wail of a car horn drifts down from the overpass and Dylan assumes any witnesses would dismiss this as homeless on homeless crime. Perhaps such a person would be so indifferent that he or she would simply look away.

As Dylan gets closer, she hears labored breath as it echoes off the wooden bench and she's no longer sure whose it is, until she hears the guy snoring. Dylan hates the sound. Her father used to snore just like that. The guy has a partially stuffed garbage bag beneath his head. Dylan hears Abby's words again, "This guy's not contributing to society and maybe he has kids he skipped out on who might benefit from any type of insurance policy a guy like him might have."

A sole streetlight shines in the cul-de-sac around the bench. It's bright except for the play of shadows obscuring the homeless man's torso. This is an unknown enemy. An innocent man. Dylan has never had cause to assault someone who posed no threat to her. That Awesome Sanchez may or may not be dead has no bearing on this: that son of a bitch had it coming. This homeless guy, though...this is different.

As Dylan walks closer, the stench of old garbage and urine emanate off the guy. Dylan's read about dumpster diving in online newspapers and the guy is obviously so much of a junkie that he's lost control of his bladder. If it were up to Dylan, she'd shake the guy awake and direct him to the burnt-out house Abby and she fled a week ago. Damaged as the house might be, it would provide more comfort than this sun-worn park bench, and Dylan no longer has any use for it.

But she doesn't say a word because she doesn't know this fucking guy, and doesn't really give a shit about him. The only threat he poses to Dylan is one of omission. Failing now will cost her everything she's come to value in this world, so she has to do it. But still, in the absence of a threat, it just doesn't seem right. As she approaches the reclined figure of the homeless man, Dylan's throat tightens as if her neck muscles were strangling her. The closer she gets, the faster blood pumps in her veins. She feels the surge of adrenaline and then cortisol. And her face and ribs fight against her. She clamps down a breath to hold and then slams the blade of the knife into an expanse of olive-green cloth between the homeless man's clavicle and right shoulder. It's a last-minute decision to give the guy a fighting chance of surviving the wound, if he can get to the emergency room in time.

The homeless man cries out, "Yeeow, Jesus!" so loud that Dylan extracts the knife and darts behind a row of hibiscus. She can't see Abby, or if the man's wailing has attracted any attention yet, but she has to get out of there. She wipes the blade with a handful of pine needles before she folds it closed and tucks it into her pocket. The homeless man cries out, "It killed me! It killed me!"

Dylan crawls through the low brush of landscaping surrounding the cul-de-sac and sees Abby waiting by the fountain, picking her nails. "Relax," she says. "No one saw a thing."

Dylan is trying to slow her breathing. "This place could be crawling with cops any minute."

"Lower your excitement level. Passersby rarely alert the authorities when they hear bums spouting off in public."

"It's not worth the risk."

"You're right," Abby says, looking over her shoulder before crossing the street. On the other side, she squeezes the knife in Dylan's pocket, stroking it like a cock. "It looked like you got him a little wide."

"No, I did it. I got him. Heard air leak out his collapsed lung." The lie cheapens it. Her excitement over the blade pushing through skin and hitting bone is reduced by half. She never wants to lie to Abby again.

Nine

While her usual technique is tactical and seductive, tonight Abby throws out any semblance of restraint. In the bunk room of the hunting shed, she pushes Dylan down and rips the fly of her pants in her urgency to get them off. There is anger in her hands and in her teeth. The drive from downtown St. Pete to the family land took forever and she can wait no longer. After tugging the khakis and underwear down to Dylan's ankles, the musky tuft of pubic hair meets her face. Bent there, she sniffs it, licks down the length to Dylan's pleasure button. She spits on it, but only to moisten it before stroking her and then squatting over her face. Abby clamps her legs and traps Dylan's head an inch from her own pleasure zone. She leans her weight back on her heels. It's the first time all week her ankle doesn't bother her, but why wouldn't it in this position? Remembering that incident reenergizes her anger and she lowers down and rides Dylan's face with abandon.

At first, Dylan is quiet, and Abby suspects she's suffering the guilt of stabbing the homeless man combined with the fear that she knows she didn't kill him like Abby asked. But after pulling her feet out from under her, she begins bouncing in bedspring symphony on Dylan's face, her ass bones pounding into her forehead. The resulting sound is wet and it makes them both moan and it is exactly what she needs right now.

After Abby's first orgasm, she slows her rhythm. Dylan's still quiet except for sporadic heavy breathing. Abby doesn't have the razor blade clamped between her teeth because she won't need that tonight. Instead, she bends forward, licks in a circular pattern, teasing. And in that position, she rocks back into Dylan's face with increasing intensity. From the pants around her left ankle, Abby pulls out the pocketknife.

Dylan squirms until her head emerges to outside of Abby's thigh. "You're not going to use that, are you?"

"Yeah." Abby breathes in Dylan's pubic hair. "It'll be hot."

"But it's got blood on it."

"So?"

"Microorganisms," Dylan says, leaning up, her face looking pained.

Abby shakes her head in disbelief.

"You know," Dylan says. "Germs."

"I know what you mean, but you worry too much."

Dylan sits there, folded at the waist, her clenching stomach muscles holding her in place as she looks up at Abby and smiles. "But still. Old habits. You know?"

Abby's not clear on her meaning, but she opens the knife and waits to see the reaction.

Dylan says, "I'm not fucking around." She pushes Abby off with a hand gripping hers, and holding the knife away, Dylan rolls them both until she's on top of Abby. With her free hand, Dylan takes the knife away, folds it, and stashes it in the nightstand drawer alongside a screwdriver and the razor blade, which she picks up and hands to Abby. Abby's winded from the struggle and it's hard to believe her heart is beating so hard in her chest. Dylan then mounts her and Abby feels her weight bearing down on her. One bead of sweat trickles off Dylan's forehead onto hers. Abby feels it hit her hairline and roll down the center of her scalp and onto the bed.

"Here," Dylan says, laying the razor blade in her palm. "You can use this." She throws Abby's legs apart and grinds her pubic hair where Abby has none. "You can cut my arm or my stomach whenever you want."

Abby resists the urge to slash Dylan repeatedly and instead

pulls at her and locks her ankles around her back. Abby wants Dylan hot and wet and she's going to drive her absolutely fucking crazy before she gets her off the best she's ever had—not because she deserves it, but because this is her last time. Final sex. Dylan doesn't deserve the bells and whistles, but it's not about her. If she had it her way, Dylan would be a man, but whatever. This is Abby's finale. Last call on center stage. With that in mind, she loosens her grip with her legs, lets Dylan have more room to rise and fall onto her. They will be dead in a matter of hours and there is no better way to spend them, and she's going to get everything she needs from this, no matter if it kills Dylan.

After her fourth orgasm, Dylan rolls off. She's breathing hard, but manages to say, "You didn't do it. Why didn't you do it?"

"I want you to watch me when I do it," Abby says, straddling her lower legs, this time facing her. She rubs the blade along the insides of Dylan's thighs and up around the pubic line. She has so many options in front of her. Above any pedestrian pleasure of sixty-nine-ing, Abby recognizes that she could cut her initials into Dylan's abdomen, or etch a picture of the room there. She could use the razor-sharp knife to amputate the nearest appendage, but that would be in no one's best interest. She runs the back of the razor blade through Dylan's curly pubic hair and then scoots up and mounts Dylan in better position to access the tender flesh on her exposed ribs. This is the perfect place to go deeper than usual, but she's determined not to get carried away. Her inner thighs are sore and she's exhausted, but she wants to make Dylan come one last time and watch her enjoy it. In a way, she's tempted to finish the job right now. She could cut into Dylan's femoral artery and then plunge the blade into her own abdomen.

But Abby doesn't feel Dylan's ready. Even if she were ready, Abby doesn't know how to spring it on her. Doesn't know if *she's* ready. Too much information too soon would be like yanking the pole and trying to set the hook too quickly. She knew she set the hook the day she got her black eye. Now she wants to reel slowly until Dylan burns the last of her denial and indignation.

Now, on the bed in the hunting shed with Dylan, her instinct is to cut deep. Get her money's worth, so to speak, but she resists. Instead, she goes thin, but long. She gets Dylan on her side and slices her, as if opening an envelope, from hamstrings up to neck. A thin ridge of blood forms like a river rising out of the desert. With her free hand, she pinches Dylan's nipple. And as always, Dylan comes forcefully immediately afterward. She's come in a forceful squirt a time or two, but not like this, and Abby loves it.

Afterward, Abby carefully bandages Dylan's new wound and checks the old ones. Her skin is raw from the adhesive side of the tape keeping her together. The older of the cuts have scabs starting to form. Abby smooths the tape surrounding Dylan's new wound and says, "Okay, get out."

"What?"

"You heard me. Get out." Abby mocks Dylan from the night they met.

Dylan's face changes and Abby doesn't like the direction it's going.

"Relax. I'm just fucking with you. I didn't mean that. I just mean, I want to take a bath and would like some privacy."

"Why?"

"Because I do."

"What are you going to do?"

"I'm going to bathe. You know, wash, rinse, repeat."

"After what we've been doing, I'd imagine you'd be less modest."

"But I'm not," Abby says. "To quote a phrase, 'because of what we've done.'"

Dylan looks angry as she rises from the bed and slips into her khaki pants.

"I'm sorry. Couldn't resist." Abby rests her hands on Dylan's shoulders, kisses her on the lips. "Seriously. I'll freshen up and then we'll get something to eat."

"That's fine."

"Shut the door on the way out."

On the couch in the big room, Dylan stretches out her legs and lets her feet rest on the hunting shed floor. The rubber soles of her shoes squeak against the cold terrazzo, but the only other sound is that of water running in the pipes that fill Abby's bath on the other side of the wall. If she would've let her, Dylan would forget about getting her new bandage wet; she'd be in there with her. Just to wash her and clean her as if she were a speedboat or a motorcycle she's ridden all day and now has to stow until next time. Dylan takes a drink of water and laughs as she replaces the cap. Comparing Abby to a recreational motor craft is laughable, until she realizes those things can kill you, too. The realization makes her uncomfortable.

Instead of getting up and seeing if she can at least wash Abby's back, Dylan pulls at the tape to her newest wound. The others are healing and the newest one fascinates her. Collagen hasn't had time to form a bridge to reconnect the separated shores of flesh. Protein fibers have yet to bond and build a scab that cocoons the skin and will become the next gossamer memento. This cut, larger in area than the others, will be influenced by the depth of the wound, but also by the blood supplied to the area. The color and thickness of her skin, as well as the direction of the blade, determines the scar's appearance.

She distracts herself by looking at the dark fireplace, which is absent of heat but ready to perform its function. Dylan loves the hunting shed. It's stark while providing all the basics of decent human existence. It reminds her of every house she's ever lived in; all those military houses she lived in while her father became the original single parent, then the Marine barracks, and finally her own house.

She focuses on the fireplace. The grate is charred from what must have been countless good times passing around a bottle or two of good bourbon, maybe even moonshine. She pictures Abby's father here with half a dozen captains of industry bragging about their kills that day during the hunt, as well as the previous weeks in boardrooms and on conference calls. Dylan squeezes the plastic water bottle she's holding and then relaxes her grip. She strangles the bottle again for a moment and then relaxes her grip. Then a third time. It calms her as she processes the anger.

Abby knows the wounds Dylan inflicted on the homeless man are superficial, and this justifies her planning an alternate course. She interpreted Dylan's inability to kill the homeless man as empathy. She knows that if Dylan has empathy enough to spare the homeless guy's life, she'll have more than enough to try to save Abby.

She wants a beer from the fridge, but the beer might as well be water from the tap. It doesn't matter; she's chasing the flavor of God.

Plan B is what she calls a fail-safe long shot. She's learned enough through the past couple of years to be more proactive. Time forces her to get creative. She can't bank on Dylan taking the pills or keeping them down. She might wait until the last second and puke them up. Abby can't go get the crossbow, because that would be difficult to turn against herself. No, this is the only way.

If she had more time, she could wait a couple days, see if Dylan comes around. Or Abby could give her another test and see if she passes. But, no. Time is up. This will be for the best, she convinces herself. She's ready and it isn't worth risking Dylan getting away. Plan B is fine. More utilitarian than glamorous, but so be it.

She thinks of the electrician she had out here a while back. His shirt with "Dan" stitched in red above the left pocket. "I didn't know they had power out here until I saw today's call sheet," Dan said. "My father had it run special before we were born," Abby replied.

After toweling off, she retrieves the screwdriver she left in the nightstand drawer, climbs upon the bed, and begins dismantling the ceiling fan's light kit. She starts with the glass dome snugged there by three small screws. Dan, the electrician, had pulled a thick black fuse with needle-nose pliers and worked his magic to fortify the circuit to withstand an electrical short much longer than normally possible.

Once she has the dome cleared, she disconnects the light bulb's mounting plate and threads her finger through the opening. She tugs at the large yellow wire nuts keeping the white wires joined together yet separate from the black wires. She is proud of her knowledge on the subject. She hadn't enjoyed researching online. Every once in a while during her five-day fact-finding mission, she thought about giving up and just asking someone, but that would make people suspicious, and she didn't want any more scrutiny than she already got on an average day. So instead of taking the easy way out, she forged on and gathered the information she needed, the lynchpin of it all coming from a chat room where she used an indecipherable alias and spoke mostly to disinterested people from Seattle and Dallas. She hopes it's enough. Hopes she's devised her plans properly.

She carefully removes the plastic wire nuts and electrical tape to expose bare wires. The room goes black the minute she removes the first wire. She carefully hops down from the bed and tosses the fixture off to the side. In the darkness, she feels around the room to find the light switch beside the door and makes sure it's off.

With the bare wires exposed, she decides that the entire situation would go smoothly if not for the obstruction of the ceiling fan. "Easy enough," she says. But then she's awkwardly aware of her nudity and resultant lack of pockets before clamping her teeth on the shaft of the screwdriver, freeing up her hands and then trying to remove the fan from its mounting bracket. Progress is slow because it's middle-of-nowhere dark in the room, and because she's never really bothered to look at how the fan had been removed from the mounting bracket. She feels two screws fastened to the ceiling and removes the screwdriver from her mouth. She hates the taste of metal. Before tackling the screws, she continues to feel around until she discovers the ball and socket design. She feels the slot on the socket and wonders if it can be that easy. "Fuck it," she says.

Climbing down, she's thrown off balance when the mattress gives beneath her and she lands awkwardly on her sore ankle. "Motherfucker," she says.

"Are you okay in there?" Dylan hollers from the living room.

Abby straightens herself. She has to think quickly. She can lie and say everything is fine, but if Dylan walks in she'll know something is seriously wrong and run for high ground. Abby's out of options, save but one. "I'll be out in a minute," she yells.

She clicks on the light in the bathroom and finds an old Igloo cooler beneath the table along the back wall and places it in the shower. The water running at full blast collides with the bottom of the empty cooler in a dangerously loud way so Abby lowers the pressure, but in addition to taking too long, it's even louder. She instead steps naked into the cooler and lets the water shower her as it fills. It only takes a few minutes, and afterward, Abby dismounts from the cooler and over the tiled ledge to land with a slight bow. She wastes no time turning to her task of hefting the whole thing out of the tub without spilling.

She squats, her knees out wide, and grasps both handles before pressing up and waddling toward the bed and setting the cooler upright beneath the light fixture in the center of the ceiling. At the bed, she knows a full splash will be too loud, so she leans the cooler, tipping it forward until water flows smoothly onto the rumpled sheets. This too makes more noise than she thinks it should, so she lies down on the bed while holding the cooler in place and then pulls it down to pour over her. In addition to deadening the noise, the rush of water feels like some sort of auto-baptism. She allows herself this before getting up to repeat the process again.

When she's done, her breath is shallow and she tries to slow it down, but excitement like this should be enjoyed.

Surely her parents will give her a funeral, probably at Goodall's. Mother wouldn't survive without the pageantry. Abby knows they'll lie about the circumstances surrounding her death, and they'll likely pay off reporters and authorities to minimize attention—just like they did in her car crash thirteen years ago. Cover the badge with green and she's off the hook. Write a check to the hospital and records are destroyed.

She closes her eyes to picture Dylan opening the door and throwing on the light to see what's going on—one hundred twenty volts will shoot through her and into the wet soles of her feet and back up through her heart and brain. Dylan'll be so panicked she'll lunge for Abby and complete the circuit and be locked to her into eternity.

If that hick of an electrician didn't fuck it up, everything should be set. She rationalizes it down to two simple facts: by choosing to save her, Dylan willingly commits suicide. It is her choice. Abby's fine with overlooking the coercion.

With the door closed and the light switch off, as well as the light in the bathroom, she rolls herself across the wet mattress and then stands up and licks her fingers before reaching overhead and into the darkness trying to find the wires. With one firmly grasped in each fist, she calls out, "Hey, Dylan. Yo, sexy. Get in here. I need something." She can see nothing but the beam of light coming from under the closed door as she listens for the sounds of Dylan's trotting feet. But there are none. "Dylan! Goddamnit. Get in here. I need your help." This time she expects the foot falls to come hard and fast, but again there is no break in the light coming from under the door and no sound of shoes on the floorboards.

She considers climbing down and peeking through the door, but decides that might seem too obvious to Dylan. Then again, if she's fallen asleep out there, she might never hear Abby.

She climbs down and cracks open the door, peeks out. The kitchen light is off, so she can only see the back of the couch from her position hugging the door. She doesn't want to call Dylan's name for fear of catching her unprepared. Instead, she goes into the bathroom and wraps herself and her hair in towels so she doesn't give herself away by dripping all over the living room floor. She then walks quietly back toward the couch and, just as she guessed, Dylan's sleeping. She apparently fell asleep while reading a copy of *Poor Richard's Almanac* because it's tilted forward, somehow balancing between her grasp and her lap.

Abby wants to hug her then, to thank her for being the one she finally conscripted to the final act. There have been dozens of others who never got this far, and she's had dozens of opportunities to convey her appreciation to Dylan as she watched her sleep, but this is it. The next time they're together will be at the end of a highly charged circuit of electricity. Hugging her now might wake her and she can't risk that. Instead, she reaches over, pulls the book from her, and then retreats toward the bunk room door. A few steps away, she tosses the book at the couch, hoping to graze Dylan's shoulder and have it land on the cushion beside her, waking her in the process. Instead, the book catches the side of Dylan's head, causing her to fall forward while exclaiming, "Oww!"

Abby sprints the few steps back to the bunk room as quietly and quickly as she can with the aggravated ankle and closes the door. Her heart beats faster than it ever has.

She springs up onto the bed and rolls around, rewetting herself like a catfish in salt water, then jumps to her feet again. The light out in the main room left her night vision further reduced, but she stands on the wet mattress and once again reaches into the darkness until she finds the exposed wires. "Hey!" she screams.

"Dylan, come here. Hurry!" and waits for her knight in scarred armor.

The book falls to the floor as Dylan jumps up in response to hearing what sounds like a scream. She's disoriented and surprised by the dull ache in her shoulder, and her first step crushes the empty water bottle beneath her foot. The next noise is partially masked by the crunch of plastic. She waits a second, on edge like a dog ready to spring into action if given the command. A moment goes by until she hears it again. This time, it's a sustained pitch followed by, "Dylan, hurry."

Dylan leaps over the back of the couch and toward the bunk room as fast as she's able. She doesn't take the time to call out or do anything but traverse that distance between them and give Abby whatever help she may need.

Dylan throws open the door to pitch-blackness. The residual light behind her illuminates only the first three feet inside the door.

Abby screams again. She's only a few feet from the door, and the sound deafens Dylan like an ice pick. She slaps the wall to find the light switch.

When she flips it on, there is no new light, but Abby's scream becomes a guttural rumble. Suddenly, her outline is visible, standing on the bed in unnatural convulsions. The air is ionized around her. She's stuck to the overhead wires and they whip her side-to-side in a convulsion of burning energy. Dylan flips off the switch and smells burning flesh in the room. With her eyes adjusting to the darkness, she searches her memory as well as the dark room for the most solid nonconductor there. She grabs the wooden chair next to the little table and pushes Abby off the charge. She falls to the floor, motionless.

Dylan slides to Abby's side on her knees. The smell of burning skin and hair is worse at this proximity. Dylan drags her toward the wedge of light near the door, and notices she's wet from head to toe. She checks Abby's pulse at the wrist. Dylan's not wearing a watch, but she can't find a pulse anyway. Abby's fingertips are disfigured, claw-like in their blackness. Dylan reaches up to test her neck and doesn't find a pulse on her first try. She sits back on her heels, trying to remember the new rules for CPR.

With stiff arms, she compresses Abby's chest, feeling her sternum dip into the cavity beneath her chest. All the while, she holds her own breath. Abby comes to with a cough and Dylan kicks herself back to the wall and finds that the floor is wet. Abby might have evacuated her bladder, but she couldn't possibly hold this much water. In her wonderment, Dylan grabs the bed and is surprised to find it too is soaked. She looks down at Abby and then up at the light fixture.

"This is it?" Dylan says. "This is the way you wanted it to go down?"

Abby shivers as if her marrow has turned to ice and her mouth is so dry she feels her chattering teeth may cause her lips to disintegrate. The breeze she feels carries opera music from the arena and the aroma of espresso and ouzo from the cafes downstairs.

"Abby," Dylan calls to her from far away.

Abby laughs because she's not in Italy and because she'll never eat or drink again. "You're supposed to come with me," she says. "It was part of the plan."

"I didn't know." Dylan leans over her. It's like old times with old boyfriends and Abby has an idea what Dylan's doing. She smooths strands of hair from around Abby's forehead and face. "I didn't know."

She's convulsing with cold as Dylan hugs her. Sweat beads on Dylan's hairline and she feels the warm air blowing in through the open window on the opposite wall, but it doesn't warm Abby.

"It's too late. You've got to take me out."

"Does it hurt?"

Abby brushes her tongue across her lips, first the top then bottom, leaving no moisture behind. "Dylan, I could have let anyone kill me. I need it to be you. Now."

Dylan breaks. Tears spill from her eyes and roll down to Abby's face. She wipes them on her shoulders as soon as they land.

Abby says, "We'll be together on the other side."

Dylan straddles Abby's torso and grips her neck, because choking is as gentle as going to sleep in comparison to the ballistic violence of something more immediate. Dylan communicates with her through their eyes, like they did when she cut her in that very room less than two weeks ago. This is more intimate and urgent.

As Dylan squeezes Abby's neck, she holds her breath and grinds her chin into her chest. The friction there on bare skin sends a flash through her like fireworks. And for a moment, it isn't Abby's face gagging beneath her hands, but her mother's. Instead of her own hands, there are smaller hands around the throat, but they clench with equal tenacity. She grips as hard as her hands allow and looks around the room to prove that she's in the bunk room with Abby, but all she sees is the little kitchen in their shitty base house in Subic Bay. The picture dissolves in a screen full of static; Abby's bucking legs require attention.

As Dylan pins down Abby's hips with her own, she tightens her grip. Abby's bucking slows and then stops. Dylan slides her feet out on either side and sees the white Nikes she got when she was fourteen. She's no longer in the bunk room but is standing on the linoleum of her mother's kitchen.

Late on the night of her birthday, when she finally came home after buying sex from a dance girl in one of the bars on the strip, her mother had waited up for her in the kitchen with a knife in her hand.

"Mom," Dylan said. "It's me. It's okay. I'm home."

"You father will strap you."

For the first time, Dylan didn't flinch when she heard that. "No, he won't," she said.

Mom walked a pace closer, gesturing with the knife in her hands. "What makes you so sure, missy?"

"I've got good news for him. That's why."

"Tell me," she said, pressing the tip of the blade into Dylan's Van Halen T-shirt.

"I won't have to take anymore beatings because I'm, I'm a woman now. I fucked a woman at the ToLo. Just like him. He won't hate me anymore."

"You," she said, leaning into Dylan as she talked between her teeth. "You and your goddamn whores."

Dylan turned away, but Mom had her pinned between the fridge and the half wall. "Stop, Mom," she called out. "You're cutting me."

"No more whores," she yelled, and cut Dylan deeper.

Sweat falls from Dylan's forehead, grazes Abby's cheek. Her convulsions have ceased and, as far as Dylan can tell, so has Abby's fight for air.

Dylan springs up from Abby's side in a spasm and instinctually grabs the chair and lifts it overhead. The chair crashes into the door and rebounds, lands on Abby's leg. Dylan punches herself in the ribs and then in the head: right fist, left fist, over and over again.

When her fists burn, she gropes against the back wall, searching for a remote sense of stabilization. Her sweat-dripping hair paints the dry white wall in sweeping arcs. Her heart is a drumroll. More than grief, more than remorse. More even than her cowardice to die—her temptation to live.

After a moment, Dylan breaks herself away from the wall. Rights herself with a push just strong enough to propel her forward.

Racing back to Abby, Dylan slides into the bed. Abby's body is reposed, wet and still warm. Dylan throws her arm over Abby's naked waist and lies her head against her shoulder, sinks her face into hers, smells her one last time, and licks the perspired salt from her lips. It tastes better than the flavor of metal in her mouth.

"I'm sorry." Dylan reaches over to the nightstand, wraps her shaking fingers around the handle of the knife as she whispers into Abby's ear. "I'm sorry." She tightens her grip, squeezes her fingers with the bone-breaking tenacity of unadulterated adrenaline.

She holds the knife out at arm's length and then presses it to her chest as if hugging it. The guilt of not jumping on that knife, impaling herself without reservation, battles for space in her brain with a sudden pride for having discovered the urge to live.

She picks up Abby's arm, gently. Kisses her hand and then gropes for a pulse. She places her fingers in various spots, searching up and down. When she finds none, she bends down and kisses her one last time. If life had handed them different cards, they could have been a couple. Maybe even living together one day. Dylan would have liked to buy her a ring. If things were different, they could have had each other to themselves. Spent a life happy together, like no one in her family ever had.

Dylan sinks to her knees. There is no way she can buy Abby that ring now, but there is one thing she can give her to symbolize their eternal union. Dylan unfolds the knife and lowers her hand down to the unobstructed target of the flawless canvas of Abby's pelvis. That blank flesh. With a continuous motion of the knife, Dylan traces the sharp point in a sideways figure eight pattern, each winding revolution pressing firmer. Deeper. They'd have no wedding rings. Never be married.

But they'd have infinity.

Dylan wakes not knowing how long she's been out. Abby is on

the bed, looking angelic.

"The first thing I should do," she says, standing and speaking to Abby's corpse as if it were the sewing form she kept in her bedroom, "is minimize evidence." She walks to the door, moves the broken chair, and opens the door wider so more light shines in. "My prints are around your neck, and my fingerprints and other assorted DNA are all about the place."

She holds her breath as she goes into the garage and finds a couple of gallons of bleach. She scrubs down Abby's neck and lifeless body. The bruises don't wipe off, of course, and she worries they might reveal her identity somehow. She has to get rid of the bruises since the bleach can't.

She removes her belt, wraps up Abby's wrists, and hauls Abby onto her feet. She hears a sound she's always associated with roosters and considers it possible that a farm is nearby.

Clenching her in one arm, Dylan reaches to thread the belt through the light fixture's mounting bracket. She fails on the first attempt and Abby slides down to the bed.

"You deserve a proper burial," she says, bending to pick Abby up again. "But this is the best I can do right now."

On the second effort, the belt threads through and she uses the leverage like a pulley, hoisting Abby high enough to fasten her with her hands above her head, within reach of the exposed wires. "The more of your skin burned, the better," she says, wrapping the bare leads around each of her index fingers.

With Abby secure there, she searches around the room, finds an old flannel shirt. She thinks of taking it to wear herself, but instead cuts it into squares and soaks them with bleach. She scrubs the doorknob on her way out to the main part of the hunting shed and wipes anything she might have touched, including the book and the crushed plastic bottle on the floor. It feels like days since she hydrated. In the bathroom, she drinks from the faucet and wipes the toilet seat and handle, rubs between each spoke of the taps. In the mirror, Abby is strung up to the ceiling in the bunk room. Dylan wipes her hands on the rag she's holding and looks at Abby. She wishes it could be some other way, but as she walks through the bunk room, she stops when she gets to the door. Stands there for a moment in silent worship. She reaches with a bleach-soaked rag over her hand on her way out and flips on the light switch.

As Dylan opens the hunting shed door, she's centered in the beam of headlights, and she hears a gunshot ring out from the general direction where Abby's car is parked. The bullet sizzles just inches past her ear. She ducks behind the oak-limb railing while Lawton police-grips his pistol, aiming right at her.

"I told you to stay the fuck away from her." Lawton fires again at Dylan, who's blinded by the headlights. She hears the bullet chunk into the wood on the railing, sending splinters into the air.

"You should have listened to me, cutter."

Dylan jumps over the railing and falls in near weightlessness as the earth is pitched and slides softly to the driveway behind the house. She feels asphalt beneath the soles of her shoes, and she reaches around until she feels the outline of the ATV Abby left parked outside the first time she'd taken Dylan there, a couple weeks ago. She ducks down. Hides. Buys herself time. As her vision returns, she takes little comfort in the shelter and braces for the next shot. Then another, and four more. Dylan hugs the machine in front of her as if imploring it to protect her, then notices the keys still in the ignition. She wonders if she can get it started in the time it takes Lawton to reload. Instead, Dylan realizes motorcycle engines can't outrun bullets.

"She's dead, isn't she?" Lawton calls.

Dylan doesn't know what to do, what to say. Before exiting the hunting shed, she'd grabbed Abby's old duffle bag and stuffed in her passport and a change of clothes. She is momentarily frozen there in a crouch. She doesn't want to say anything to incriminate herself, and running will only give Lawton a clearer target.

"It was beyond my control."

"Bullshit."

"You knew her, man," Dylan says as her musculoskeletal system protests the crouched position. Her lung capacity is in Olympic-athlete condition, but her leg muscles are trained for linear movement, like the treadmill and elliptical machine in her home gym, not the physical demands of evading the gunfire of a madman. All these squatting and lateral movements are foreign to her, and are made more of a challenge beneath the weight of the duffle bag and her all-encompassing grief.

"Fuck!" Lawton hollers. "I need to visit Awesome Sanchez. I need to get high."

Dylan, in some minute way to make it up to him, wants to save him the trip. "Awesome Sanchez might be dead."

"You killed him, too?"

"I might have. He was insulting Abby."

"Oh, that's just great." Lawton switches to a side-facing position, pointing the gun with one outstretched arm. "Come on out of hiding. Make this easier on yourself and I'll kill you quickly."

Dylan realizes it would be justice in many ways, but she can't do it.

Lawton slams another magazine into his pistol. "She's been planning this for years. I just really hoped she'd keep putting it off."

Dylan's stomach is knotted and her brain is twisting in her skull.

"You're not getting away with this."

"It was her decision, man. If it wasn't me, it would have been somebody else."

"If it wasn't you, she'd still be alive." Lawton squeezes off another round.

Dylan hops from the shadows and takes off running. Lawton gets off two more shots, and the nearby roosters clamor in unison with the explosions ringing in Dylan's ears.

The shots come close in succession and proximity; one not more than a foot away from her ear, the next landing near her foot as she darts toward the pond. Dylan hears Lawton's footfalls in the brush behind her. To avoid giving herself away with a splash, Dylan crawls into the pond on her belly, dragging her legs behind. The sand is thick and muddy and sucks at her hands and her knees as she drags herself as silently as possible into the ink-black water. As she makes her way headfirst into the pond, she hopes Lawton won't shoot her in the ass or take off a foot with that Glock he's blasting around. Dylan's surprised the water is so much colder than the outside air, but she doesn't hesitate. She crawls and then walks deeper, until her head is just above the surface. She inhales as big a breath as she can silently take.

She's finally able to utilize the skills she picked up while in the Corps, training in dense vegetation at Fort Story. And though it's been twenty years since her training at Camp Mackall, she needs all the skills she can recall.

The dark water is even colder beneath the surface than she anticipated, and the weight of the flooded duffle bag strapped across her torso makes her sink to the bottom, slowly like a bloated turtle.

Evading capture and survival came naturally and the duffle bag she has now is a fraction the size of the deuce gear she trained with in that North Carolina swamp. She's free to swim and slither to a thicket of reeds fifty yards from shore, which serves as her fighting hole. Her line of sight is strong at first, but Lawton moves around spastically, firing wildly at the water.

If she were not evading death by bullet, she'd surely never risk the bone-crunching jaws of any number of alligators sure to be in this very water.

From day one, Lawton knew that no good could come from knowing that cutter. "Okay, cutter," he says. "I warned you,

you cunt." Lawton waves the Glock in the air. "Come on out from there. I've got to put two bullets in your head and get you over to the hog swamp on the other end of the property."

Dylan doesn't respond, but the shadows move and then Lawton hears the faint trickling of water and knows what she's doing.

He fires into the water. Waits and then fires twice more. He wants Dylan dead, but more than that, he wants to make enough noise to wake Abby. To bring her back.

The reeds are thin and Lawton waits, knowing the bitch will make noise as she surfaces to take another breath.

"I'll fucking kill you!" he yells. Rage has him squeezing the pistol in his hand, and he fires three more times into the water before sadness causes him to fold up on himself with a whimper, softly at first, which leads into sobs and then, a full-out cry. His throat closes up, but his eyes and nose are pipelines for voluminous snot and tears.

After smearing his face with the backs of his hands, Lawton cranes his neck to put one ear closer to the pond. He still hears nothing and assumes that he might have gotten the bitch with one of his shots. It isn't unreasonable to believe a shot or two got an artery or some vital organ as the bitch ran away. It's also possible that her body won't surface, especially if she sank in the thick bottom mud.

But then Lawton thinks Dylan might have silently swum across to the other side and taken off running into the night. "Son of a bitch!" he yells, then fires twice more, emptying his gun in her general direction. When he stops to reload, he drops the magazine from his back pocket. As he bends to retrieve it, a fat gator belches a hiss through open jaws, which close around his foot, and then his leg, and then, somehow, both legs.

Dylan emerges at the surface behind reeds on the other side and recycles her air. Her ears are caked with mud and tiny fish swim in her pants, but she hears no more gunfire. Dylan sidesteps to the center of the reeds and remains ducked down. She shivers and her teeth chatter, but she extracts herself from the gooey pond floor and walks to the shore. Black water as viscous as motor oil soaks her to the marrow and has flooded the duffle bag, weighing her down by a number of pounds. It's a struggle to make it out onto dry land, and she stops for a moment to let the bag drain a little. What really makes walking difficult are the slimy patches of algae from the pond floor sticking to the bottoms of her shoes.

In her mind, it's only a matter of time before Lawton discovers the crossbow.

Dylan takes off in the direction she surmises is east, sloshing the bag behind her. The knife Abby gave her is in her pocket instead of holstered there upside down like her Ka-Bar, but it's the only weapon she'll need.

Looking over her shoulder periodically, she puts distance behind her, makes her way to the bus station downtown. She's dried off during the walk, but she's dirty and surprised so many people are there at that time of night. She feels all their eyes on her. Weaving through the crowd, they are all obstacles, and what's worse, she feels they know what she has done. Even those not paying attention to her surely suspect the crimes she's guilty of. She knows they can smell death on her hands.

She boards the first bus leaving, and with a shaking hand on the handrail pulls herself aboard in a heave of exhaustion. Everything in her runs contrary. Fear has drained all moisture from her muscles. Her legs are useless. Her bones are burnt wood. Guilt sucks the blood from her heart as it pounds too fast despite the canals shattered throughout.

She heaves the duffle bag onto the top step and struggles to follow it up. The resulting momentum, labored as it is, propels her up. With one deflated limb rising up after the next she collapses into the first open seat in front of her. She is on. On her way.

The chatter of people in the depot, the resulting noise of

conversations amongst the stampede of nighttime travelers and those there to say goodbye, stays behind.

She should have reverberated with remorse. Should be doubled over, rocking on her heels as she sobs, but she can't force herself to do it. The sense of loss doesn't just hit her, it burrows through.

Dylan hears silence in that brief instant before the explosion of air from the brakes; the screech of metal on metal announces the closing of the door, signaling their departure. As the bus rolls smoothly from the depot, a convulsion grips her abdomen, then bends her upward like an empty can. She doesn't know where she's going. A stranger is behind the wheel and could be taking her anywhere. There is no need to look on the ticket because she doesn't have a destination in mind or a map with her to chart their progress. With the ticket in her pocket, she has four fifty-dollar bills left.

Dylan grows tired and she's too drained to fight it. She unclenches. Releases. Exhausted.

Lying in that fallen position, slumped forward across two seats, she closes her eyes. But instead of darkness, she sees it all again, a mental broadcast of the whole thing. Bullets of sweat from her throbbing face absorb into the soiled fabric of the window seat.

The acidic sting of bile fills her throat. A burst of scalding liquid rockets up her esophagus, fills her mouth from the inside; by some miracle of reflex, she manages to clamp her jaw in time, just before those liquids mix with her sweat on the foul seat fabric. She chokes it back. Swallows. The burn amplifies on the return path.

And Abby.

Abby.

Without control, without any amount of her own faculties present to stop it, Dylan jellies out, adds the liquid of pain as tears deluge the area her sweat dampens. The convulsions of her inhalations are twice as loud as the burst of her sobs. After tortured moments pass, Dylan feels a kick at the bottom of her foot.

"You okay, lady?" The voice comes out in forced breaths, as if he were barking in a whisper.

"What?" Dylan groans out the word before amending it. "*Que?*"

The man is another passenger, two rows back, in his sixties, wearing a print shirt most likely from the big and tall store nearest a buffet. After clearing his throat in a jagged roar, he removes his glasses and says, "I asked you if you were okay."

"*No Ingles,*" Dylan says to the seat through crossed arms.

The man smacks one hand against a Bible in the other. "Right."

Then Dylan sees Abby's face again, lifeless beneath her hands.

Cleve arrives at the hunting shed in time to hear gunshots and yelling. He ducks and hides behind the door of his old Crown Vic, trying to get a view of things from there. After the gunshots and yelling stop, the sound of a man's screams filled the air. When Cleve turns on his flashlight, the beam is as impotent as he and there are no extra batteries. He can't see much of anything out there, so he goes into the hunting shed to look for another light, or at least some batteries.

Once inside, he discovers a light switch, but no power. Making his way with the dim glow from his flashlight, he finds the breaker box melted in the garage. Something caused an overload he guesses, and as he continues his search for batteries or a lantern, he comes upon a body strung up to the ceiling in the bedroom. Even with his failing light and weakening eyesight, he recognizes it as a human body. He climbs up on the bed and shines the light directly into the face, recognizes Abby. Cleve drops his light, falls to his knees there on the bed, and cries at her feet.

It is nearly dawn when he stops his mourning, goes outside, and discovers the Stratton boy's torso and the bloated carcass of an alligator on the pond shore. Birds had gotten Lawton's eyes, but he recognizes the face from the mug shots he'd seen from Lawton's DUI at twenty-two. He looks the same, except for the eyes. A 9mm is still in Lawton's hand; his perfect aim had come too late.

Ten

Amongst cabbage palms and palmetto bushes in South Florida, Dylan stands in a thin tank top, enjoying the last moments of a break from digging postholes for an ostrich farmer's fence. Sweat pours from every follicle, and she feels water welling up beneath the layers of thickening hair on her head. Her tanned skin blends with the coarse bandage on the center of her chest, and is now receptive to the harsh April sunlight she's squinting into. Dylan spits a dusty ball of phlegm, then returns to kicking her shovel into limestone bedrock. It's the most alive she's felt in almost a year.

The new wound is a sizzling trail of ants as the crude burlap and duct tape bandage acts as a magnifying glass while she contracts the muscles required for manual labor.

With the heat cooking her wound like a brisket in a convection oven, sweat threatens to loosen the tape that holds the bandage to the taut skin over her heart as the sluiced meat throbs with every contraction of her arms. This stinging new wound is deep and will scar better than most of the others. Without shame, without rehabilitation. A Parnassian master swapping pain for poetry.

She'd turned forty-one the previous night, when she'd taken the soft white span of skin and, staring into the mirror, began the angled lines to carve an "A" taller and wider than any other scar before to create an entirely new scar—one larger and deeper than ever before. Doing so took more time and more passes than she'd thought, but she knew the value of the work—worth the pain now pulsating in spasms of protest—so she took her time, did it in small doses and drank water between passes, dabbed away the blood at each break. A new ritual that kept her on schedule, one she will keep.

Near the banks of Lake Okeechobee, she kicks her shovel into earth, piles up mounds of sand and muck for every fence post hole she digs. She's grateful she's free in her life as a laborer. The only item she misses from those liquidated from the abandoned house is her mother's sewing form, and there is no way to carry it around even if she had it.

The farmer who hired her almost a year ago speaks fluent Cracker, but Dylan replies only in broken English, each word so obfuscated with fake accent that the farmer requires a translator. Dylan owes her knowledge of Spanish to her father getting stationed at Roosevelt Roads, Puerto Rico for a couple of years. She's grateful for that now. It aids her cover on the lam as Dione Rivera.

The translation tandem of farmer and daughter pay Dylan more than enough to live a life of stealth. The work is good and solid, and she's vowed not to quit, no matter how hard the farmer drives her. This much she owes not only the farmer, but also herself, and more importantly, Abby. Last night marked a year to the day since she'd met her. She'd quit on Abby, and she'll never forgive herself or quit on anybody again.

Dylan kicks her shovel in deep enough to stand on its own, stretches her back into a reverse crescent, and swipes her head with a rag wedged in her pocket.

Just then, a woman appears a few posts down the line. Her black hair is slicked back, wet from a shower or a swim in the pool by the main house. Her white cotton dress is translucent and sticks to her skin like the rolling papers Abby had long ago twisted into a joint. But this woman isn't Abby. This woman's face is too round and too soft. Her breathing too shallow. Her hair too black, too widespread. She isn't even close. But last night, she didn't have to be. The woman has pursued Dylan periodically for the past year, and Dylan took her up on it because last night the woman couldn't distract her from envisioning Abby. Birthday forty-one and she was number twenty-seven.

But where the dim light of the room had flattered her, the bright light of day mocks her. Dylan doesn't want to talk. She has to finish planting these fence posts so she can prime and paint the farmer's barn before darkness sets in.

The woman steps a pace closer, and behind her a nondescript sedan drives up the path to the main house. Faint trails of dust rise from the tires along the dirt road. A lone old man exits the car, his orthopedic shoes sure-footed on the gravel drive. Dylan doesn't recognize him, but she gets an uneasy feeling as the guy stands there talking to the farmer.

Dylan picks up the shovel and then plants it firmly into the sandy ground again.

She's long ago burned her wallet and all identification, and the old duffle bag is worthless to her now; there are no items, either sentimental or otherwise, that she can't get by without. The only thing she truly needs is the knife in her pocket.

The woman reaches up and touches Dylan, her soft hand against the darkening bandage on her chest. She knows nothing of the dirt or the blood. "What happened to your chest?"

"That man walking up to your house wants to take me away. You don't want me to go away, do you?"

"Oh *Dios mio*, no. No."

"Your father won't tell him I'm here, will he?"

She hugs Dylan hard and says, "My father is unable to bring me many gifts, but he would never pull one from my hands."

ACKNOWLEDGMENTS

Tremendous debts of gratitude are owed to many people who helped or at least humored me during the writing of this book and others. Instrumental in this process were (and continue to be) Tracy Crow and James R. Duncan, who have been deeply patient, helpful, and inspirational. To Mark Fleeting, Pinckney Benedict, Fred Leebron, who praise and chide and are never wrong. To Kevin C. Jones for making me think about this one from a different angle. To my badass cousins Tommy Hess and Pete Knapp for their expertise and all else. To Steph Post, Jim Thomsen, Tim Bazzett, Phil Jason, Matt Flaherty, Mike Kobre, Chris Tyler, Tim Wright, Carol Dee Turner, Aramis Calderon, and everyone in the DD-214 Writers' Workshop, the Queens University MFA program, as well as many of the journal and magazine editors who've published my stories, essays, and articles, particularly: Jonathan Sturak and Eddie Vega at *Noir Nation*; Anthony Neil Smith at *Plots with Guns*; Steve Weddle at *Needle: A Magazine of Noir*; Nicholle M. Cormier at *The MacGuffin*; Jerri Bell and Ron Capps at *O-Dark-Thirty*; Jon Chopan, Tracy Crow, and Cliff Garstang at *Prime Number*; Mary Akers at *r.kv.r.y.*; Ralph Pennel at *Midway Journal*; to Eric Beetner for including me in the *Unloaded* anthology and Ron Earl Phillips at *Shotgun Honey*; Dr. John Fleming and the staff at *Saw Palm: Florida Literature and Art*, Lawrence Kelter with *The Black Car Business*, Ryan Sayles with *Grease Paint and .45s*, Josh Pachter with *The Great Filling Station Holdup*. (It's my sincere hope that everyone reads all these fine publications.) I'm immensely thankful to Eric Campbell, Lance Wright, and everyone at Down & Out Books. I don't know what the odds are that we'd live in the same town, but that makes this even more special to me. I'm also thankful to Zach McCain for another kickass cover, and to Elizabeth White for some mighty-fine guidance, as well as to Emily Bell, Dan Wickett, Donald Maas, and Lorin Oberweger for their insights along the way. Also to the assorted crime writers and readers with whom I've connected in various capacities online and in person. I'd also like to thank those whose presence influenced me in the early years of this adventure: James O'Neil; Willie Reader; my third-grade teacher, Mrs. Dickerson; Ronald "Bo" Walston; the Wilsons of Mobile, Alabama; Mark Amen; Mark August; Lyn Biliteri; H. Kermit Jackson; Ty Jones; Denny Sawyer; my Navy buddies, Joe Paul, Curt Jarrett, John Louthan, Perry Chastain, James "Bubba" Smith, Scott Dickerson, and all the San Jacinto Plank Owners; and my lifelong friends who are like brothers to me, Jeff Prince, Chris Hartnett, Anthony Acitelli, William Barnes, David (Hezy) Hemed, Paul Drew, and Kurt Hopson. And I'm forever thankful for my sister Cindy, Stan, Carrie, Steven, Robyn, and my entire family, but especially my parents, Carol and Jack, who showed me the way and kept me on the path. The biggest thanks of all goes to my beautiful and infinitely understanding wife, Lauren, who got on this roller-coaster with me when I thought it would be easy and loved me even after finding out that it never is. I wouldn't trade you for anything in the world!

JEFFERY HESS is the author of the novels *Scar Tissue, Roughhouse, Tushhog, Beachhead,* and *No Salvation,* and the short story collection *Cold War Canoe Club* as well as the editor of the award-winning *Home of the Brave* anthologies. He lives and writes in Florida, where he leads the DD-214 Writers' Workshop for military veterans.

JefferyHess.com

BOOKS

On the following pages are a few
more great titles from the
Down & Out Books publishing family.

For a complete list of books and to
sign up for our newsletter,
go to DownAndOutBooks.com.

Bad Guy Lawyer
Chuck Marten

Down & Out Books
March 2022
978-1-64396-249-8

The only time Guy McCann stops talking is when he's downing scotch. Guy was a hot-shot attorney for the West Coast mafia until he got cold feet and split town, earning a target on his head. Now he's lying low in Las Vegas, giving back-room legal advice to second-rate crooks while pining over his old girlfriend Blair, a working girl with a razor wit and zero inhibitions.

When Blair is committed to a psychiatric ward, Guy is drawn back to the dangerous underworld of Los Angeles. Next thing he knows, Blair has escaped from the hospital and Guy's former mafia associates are on her trail, with Guy caught in the crossfire.

Groovy Gumshoes
Private Eyes in the Psychedelic Sixties
Edited by Michael Bracken

Down & Out Books
April 2022
978-1-64396-252-8

From old-school private eyes with their flat-tops, off-the-rack suits, and well-worn brogues to the new breed of private eyes with their shoulder-length hair, bell-bottoms, and hemp sandals, the shamuses in Groovy Gumshoes take readers on a rollicking romp through the Sixties.

With stories by Jack Bates, C.W. Blackwell, Michael Bracken, N.M. Cedeño, Hugh Lessig, Steve Liskow, Adam Meyer, Tom Milani, Neil S. Plakcy, Stephen D. Rogers, Mark Thielman, Grant Tracey, Mark Troy, Andrew Welsh-Huggins, and Robb White.

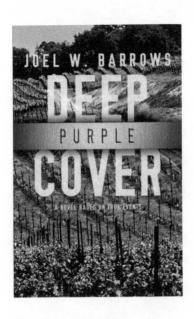

Deep Purple Cover
The Deep Cover Series
Joel W. Barrows

Down & Out Books
May 2022
978-1-64396-263-4

Things in Napa Valley are not as they seem. Everyone wants to get into the wine business, but at what cost?

When the co-owner of Pavesi Vineyards goes missing there are few clues to his disappearance. When his remains unexpectedly turn up, dark forces loom large.

FBI Special Agent Rowan Parks is assigned to the case and quickly realizes that the Bureau needs someone on the inside. There is only one person to call, her former lover, and ATF's greatest undercover operative, David Ward.

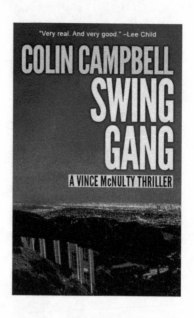

Swing Gang
A Vince McNulty Thriller
Colin Campbell

Down & Out Books
June 2022
978-1-64396-268-9

Titanic Productions has moved to Hollywood but the producer's problems don't stop with the cost of location services.

When McNulty finds a runaway girl hiding at the Hollywood Boulevard location during a night shoot e takes the girl under his wing but she runs away again.

Between the drug cartel that wants her back and a hitman who wants her dead, McNulty must find her again before California wildfires race towards her hiding place.